RED LADY
An Arcane Court Novel

By

GRAYLIN FOX

Red Lady:
The Second Arcane Court Novel

Copyright 2014 by Dark Fantasy Press

ISBN: 978-0-9899610-9-7

Published by Dark Fantasy Press

<u>Arcane Court</u>
Death Dealer
Red Lady
Demon Child
<u>Upcoming:</u>
Shadowed Vengeance – 2105
Fanged Deception - 2016

GraylinFox.com
Twitter: GraylinFox
Facebook: GraylinFoxWrites

Chapter One

"Get up, you fucking, ugly ass excuse for a dragon! I leave you for a hundred years and you move into a mansion? You've gone soft, Cimmerian."

My ex-fiancée in my bedroom—this was going to be a bad day. "Tanith, so nice to wake to your screeching. I'd forgotten what it felt like to hate my life from the instant I gained consciousness."

The shift to dragon took me moments as I rolled out of bed to stand to my full 6'11 dragon height. As a human, I stood 6' 6.

"Men and size. Did you get Wretch to spell you taller?"

She spoke with effort and, for the first time in years, I looked at the face of the only woman I'd ever considered marrying.

She stood with pride and elegance in every sinew, her normally translucent white skin marred with weeping wounds, her waist-length, natural red hair I loved matted to her head.

My shift back to human took place quickly as I ran to her side. "What happened?"

"Sex game gone crazy. You know how that is," she said with effort. The lie didn't make it to her eyes.

I'd play along. "You show up in my bedroom wounded from rough sex? Fucking demons again?"

"Yeah, they wanted to whip me until I couldn't shift." Her grip on the doorjamb loosened.

I put an arm around her. First time we'd touched since our wedding night a hundred years before. Then, she'd been astride me in bed, sweating profusely while ripping scales from my chest to get to my heart.

Her smell struck me as off. "You stink."

"You still love me. If getting my ass beat was what it took, I could've paid for Wretch to do it decades ago."

She sounded scared. I needed to know why. I'd missed her Scottish accent. Gathering her in my arms, I carried her to the bathroom.

"Uh, Boss?" George appeared in the doorway. He'd proved light on his feet for a lowland gorilla shifter. "Do we need Angie, or are you good?"

"You have quite the menagerie." Her normal acrid tone had softened; probably by her wounds.

"Call Wretch. Tell him Tanith's back, in bad shape, and to bring Angie." I kicked open the bathroom door. "Make sure he shows up with clothes on." He loved making her blush.

I had to admit she looked good with pink cheeks. Setting her down, I grabbed a washcloth.

"Who's Angie?" Tanith held onto the counter while I turned on the water.

"Wretch's human on and off girlfriend." I began to remove her clothing.

Her back, covered with welts from a whip, looked swollen, oozing puss. The infected wounds prevented her from shifting. Our systems wouldn't allow us to change shape with foreign objects or substances on our skin. The shift would distribute them to vital organs and our bloodstream—a knife may start out in your back and end up in your heart.

She laughed so hard she started to cough. "He has a human girlfriend?"

"Of course I do, you obnoxious bitch." Wretch casually walked in, his long hair sticking up, sleep framing his hazel eyes. At least, he'd covered his naked human form with a robe, barely.

Angie—human, curvy, and pissed—pushed past him. "Shut up. We have an open relationship. He sleeps around, I sleep around, and we all get laid regularly."

Her long brown hair smelled like shampoo, her ample figure dressed professionally, telling me she didn't stay with Wretch last night. Angie worked as the Chief Coroner here in New Orleans. She had a secondary lab in the basement of this house for her demon DNA injection research. He'd brought her without the new werewolf assistant.

Her exclusivity with Wretch, after her ordeal escaping a deranged pediatrician, lasted twenty-four hours. George and I had placed bets on how long he could wait before he slept with someone else. I won. A millennium of being a demon slut wouldn't disappear overnight, even if he did love the doctor.

He also did it to push her to safety. I stared at proof in front of me—knowing us came at a cost. Tanith winced. Angie examined her, shooing us out of the room.

"Let me guess. You flew to Vegas without telling me and picked her up at work?" Wretch moved to one of the couches in my huge room. He waved his hand, dressing himself in respectable clothing.

He stood six feet tall with dark blond hair to his shoulders and hazel eyes. His demon mother and dragon father would be proud; he could do demon magic with dragon strength and scales.

His family feared him. They should. It's why they hunted us.

Hard for me to remember that as he sprawled on my couch dressed in what I called his demon dandy look—linen pants with a buttoned-down shirt, undone to mid-chest. He no longer wore the gold chains around his neck after a demon damn near yanked his head off with them, decapitation being the only way to kill demons, and Wretch.

"I woke up to her screeching. What the hell was she doing in Vegas and how did you know where she was?" Now I was pissed at him.

I spelled some clothes for myself. As a dragon that sucked down demon souls at the moment of their death, I had gained the ability to do spell work. Clothing proved my limit, thus far.

He looked sheepish.

That was new. "You checked up on my ex?"

He fiddled with his collar. "She tried to rip your heart out. I soiled a good shirt before I put you back together. It was in my best interest to know where she was at all times."

"Demon contacts?"

"You bet." He smiled at me and vanished.

"Ass." The one ability I wanted to have and didn't.

He'd told me he'd help me with it, but the fear of not reappearing or coming back without my favorite parts made me limit my travels to cars, legs, or wings.

Shouts erupted in the bathroom. Well, I now knew where he went.

"So, the two of you?" George came back clothed and washed up. His hair was black with some gray in it, cropped close to his head, his eyes dark brown, almost black. At a little over six feet tall and with a football linebacker build, he had enough body hair to be accurately categorized as furry.

I had to tell him the truth at some point. "We were going to be married. She left me at the altar. Something about the company I keep."

A century later and the memories still tweaked my emotions. I left out the heart-ripping part. It hurt more. If he didn't hear Wretch mention it, I wasn't going to bring it up.

He smiled. "She's back."

"It's because she'll blame us for what happened." Nothing new there.

"What's the probability of that?"

"North of ninety-five percent." *More like ninety-nine percent.*

"Oh."

"Obsidian said she'd stay out of New Orleans. While that keeps us safe as long as we don't leave, we have family, friends, and other all over the world." It looked like she might be after them. I wanted to call my parents.

Wretch's grandmother showed up in New Orleans recently after we stopped demons from dismembering humans for body parts. Swallowing the soul of her son-in-law, Narran, as it wriggled in fury had boosted my dragon height by six inches. His wife, Nitha, lay imprisoned in an oubliette in Europe. We lost two great werewolves to Obsidian before she left. All of us were lucky to be alive—Wretch's family tree was twisted and sick at the roots.

George fidgeted. "Is my family safe?"

A reasonable question.

"They should be. In the centuries we've been fighting, no one has ever gone after my parents or extended family. Either there's a code we don't know about, or Wretch and I keep getting between demons and their desire to rule the human race as overlords."

"That's dramatic." He reached for his phone.

"And accurate." I should retire to Tahiti. Demons couldn't swim.

Wretch reappeared. "There's a large drug ring operating in Las Vegas. Her boyfriend is involved. He vanished. She traced his phone to a warehouse and was jumped by demons. They knew she was coming."

"A trap." That surprised me. "Not us?"

"You know, it's not always us." Even he sounded doubtful.

It was "us" so often; to assume otherwise could be fatal. "No, but usually, it is."

He smiled at me. "Angie said she'll heal fine. There isn't any infection, just dirt and dust in the wounds. Once she's showered, she can shift until there isn't a trace left."

I fixated on something else. "She's dating a drug dealer?"

Surprise there, Tanith being a health nut. She ate all organic foods and did yoga twice a day. I appreciated the flexibility. Or, I used to.

Wretch shook his head. "He didn't know, either. Apparently, the operation is extensive and includes the energy drinks and bars at his local gym. The hallucinations tipped Tanith off. Seems this drug allows humans to see paranormals; shifters can see demons; everyone can see demons as they appear."

George coughed. "It would be a demon shooting gallery." His attempt to hide a smiled failed.

"Yes, it would." I mulled the information over. "A gym rat."

Wretch stared at me. "Nice way to keep focus. He's human, Cim. Tanith would kill him in—"

"Shut up, Wretch." Tanith and I split up a century ago but that didn't mean I wanted to picture her in bed with someone else.

"You pushed me into Angie," he teased.

"No, you wandered that way when you damn near died, twice. Then you slept your way out of it." He'd done that to her twice now, and she still didn't tell him to fuck off.

He looked at me and, for the first time, I saw fear in his eyes. Loving us got your heart broken and then you died a horrible death by demon. We'd both kept our hearts free since my wedding night. At least, I had.

"She's safer without you. Yes," I said under my breath.

"It hurts, Cim. She got it right away. Called me on it. Told me I didn't have to break her heart to keep her safe. I don't know if I could send her out of town. But if this drug problem shows up here, I'll send her to Canada."

His family was going to succeed in making him miserable. Just not the way they planned.

"If it's not my family, you know who it is," he continued.

I ignored that for a moment. "Humans' drug reaction, specifically?"

If this drug got into the hands of street dealers, we'd have an epidemic. Shifters loved trying drugs. Our immune systems' ability to make the effects of even the harshest drugs minimal allowed for extensive experimentation, or weeklong parties, either way.

"Humans start out on a great drug trip and wind up psychotic, within days," Tanith answered from the bathroom doorway, Angie standing behind her.

"Fuck." George, this time.

I nodded. Obsidian was the strongest demon we knew, and Wretch's grandmother. His Aunt Nitha, just as deadly and psychotic, loved to kill anything with a pulse, preferably in a way to make the releasing soul scream in terror.

Wretch's family tree grew crazy and, demons being immortal, this created a problem. You had to kill them. Their souls, putrid and green, screamed out of their bodies, mourning over the loss. That was when I drank in their souls, gaining the demon's inherent magic for myself.

Days ago, I killed Narran, Nitha's husband. We still reeled from the losses inflicted by Obsidian.

Demon DNA injections... What the fuck had she started? Could this be what Tanith's boyfriend stepped in?

It wouldn't be that far-fetched. Las Vegas being a demon hub, gambling ran in their blood. Putting a lab in that area to test their injections would be a good business move. George was walking proof they could create a shifter from a genetically tough human.

Greg, my new werewolf guardian, gained size in wolf form with regular injections, making him the largest wolf we'd ever come across. Fighting by their side reminded me how powerful Obsidian would become if shifters felt they owed her for their new abilities.

Making the drug addictive significantly increased the loyalty potential. If it was sold to humans, it would decimate them, I was sure of it. The ability to see paranormals either led to understanding, or death. Death would get my vote, after rioting and gangs of humans hunting us with shotguns and automatic weapons.

The head demon drug dealer was Kragen. Over a thousand years old, he'd been selling organic hallucinogens in the dark ages. He'd proved brilliant and ruthless. If he and Obsidian set aside their mutual hatred, we'd need every dragon in the field. Even then, I'm not sure we could stop them.

"All healed up," Angie announced. "There were drugs in her wounds, likely put there by the whips used on her back. She's beautiful, Cim."

"I know, Angie. Thank you." I kissed her forehead before passing her to Wretch who vanished with her.

Tanith crawled into my bed. "I *am* beautiful, you arrogant, sexy prick. But I can't compete with demon strength."

"Just make yourself comfortable." I liked how she looked there.

"Shut up. I have a boyfriend to go back to after I rest."

Something she wasn't telling me, though

"What's his number?" It would be an odd conversation, but if calling kept him from showing up at my house looking for her, I'd make it.

"I don't know. It's programmed into my phone. Which is in pieces in the desert where I was jumped and left for dead. Go away. He's been captured, or killed by now. I'll find him when I get home."

"Let me guess, it's the drugs," George said as we walked downstairs.

"No, that's her personality." I ignored his laugh.

"Breakfast?" George asked.

"Yes, food sounds great."

Chapter Two

He cooked a buffet amount of food that we piled into two serving bowls. Our shifter metabolisms required large amounts of sustenance. We walked out to the back yard through the kitchen exit, down the wraparound porch steps, to a picnic table he'd built from recycled wood.

"This is a very nice table. Large enough for us even when we shift." Although I doubted it would support me in dragon form.

"I didn't plan that when I built it, but it works. Thanks."

We ate in silence. The sounds of animals traipsing through the bushes behind the yard calmed me. I'd been raised in a jungle; wildlife, especially small animals, let me know no predators were around. The house on the other side of the hedge sat empty. I believed some of Laythe's top bodyguards used to live there. Since her mother decapitated her in the basement, and after I took over the house, her loyal demons left town.

Tanith had returned, though. Maybe only for today, but it did prompt me to take mental note of everyone I knew outside of the New Orleans area. My parents knew of Wretch's family and were alert in case these showed up in their world travels. I'd never worried about more than five individuals at any time. Tanith being more skilled in hand to hand fighting than I was, her safety would be her concern. She insisted.

I didn't want to check out the drug trade in Las Vegas. However, it walked into my bedroom this morning, so I would. We needed to burn down any warehouses and storage facilities, and find out who ran it. Demon families were arranged like the human mafia; or, more correctly, Italian mob members tailored their organizations after the demon families who started their businesses.

Our jobs with the Arcane Court were simple. Enforce the laws, mostly to protect humans, and kill anyone who violates the law. When Obsidian signed an agreement to stay out of New Orleans for two hundred years, she'd left our local group of shifters and demons shattered. The police chief and his pack's alpha dismembered and left on my marble foyer floor proved the final deaths we linked directly to her.

George helped Grace, a jaguar shifter, run our paranormal-only club a block from the Mississippi River. Like me, she grew up in the jungles of Mexico.

"It's not quiet," George said, finishing his eggs.

"I had ten years of quiet before Nitha and Obsidian walked back into our lives. It looks like it was the last vacation I'll get until they're both dead."

Luring them here would put everyone in danger and yet, give me the best chance of killing them. Nitha was imprisoned in a European oubliette guarded by other demons. Her mother had left her there.

"Can you kill an Arcane Court member?"

That had only come up once. "They're only as immortal as their species. Being appointed doesn't grant you immunity or immortality. If they step over the line, we can kill them. Obsidian, though, didn't kill or maim humans. She's very careful. Her human husband, Dr. Brun, did. Our rules don't apply to him. Even though he injected himself with demon DNA, like you, he was categorized by the Court as human. If he'd survived our adventure, we wouldn't have been able to touch him."

He looked worried. "Could they fire Wretch for killing Brun?"

"Yes, but they won't. He had human children strapped to a table. They're going to ignore his death." The report, complete with Wretch's extensive surveillance videos, gave the Court enough to keep him employed.

The demon council had heard of Laythe's murder by her mother's hand. They'd contacted Wretch to let him know his inheritance got transferred immediately after her death. The demon-dragon hybrid I called my best friend and partner now had more money than we could spend, and we're immortal.

I needed information on the drug operation in Vegas. The best way to get intel from demons would be during a poker game, listening to them brag. With humans, I could ply them with alcohol. Not demons. Alcohol didn't affect paranormal systems. We got a slight buzz, no matter how much we consumed. Demons could spell the liquor and get wasted. The younger demons loved to stumble drunk down Bourbon Street.

"I'll be playing poker tonight."

"Want backup?" George asked, smiling.

"I'm not planning on getting spelled human again." The last time I played poker with demons, they spelled me human and I ran down Bourbon Street at three in the morning, nude. No one except Wretch noticed.

George cleaned up the mess in the kitchen while I leaned against the counter pretending it didn't bother me. He insisted on doing everything because I let him live here for free. It was Laythe's home and Wretch had inherited it. He gave it to me. His place sat on the other side of Jackson Square behind a nondescript-looking blue fence—a place worth millions, and he'd lived there for two hundred years. Like my club, he could vanish there and reappear and I could shift and fly away.

"I smell food." Greg stood in the doorway. He was my human form height, six-foot-six-inches, and shifted into a wolf whose haunches reached my hip. He had wild, dark-blond hair, and blue eyes. Most women melted when he entered a room. He never noticed.

George pointed the sleepy werewolf to the coffee while he made another batch of ham steaks, eggs, and sausages. Greg cleaned his plate, burping loud enough for me to feel it.

I held my breath for a moment. "Nice one."

"So, the smoking-hot redhead in your bed. Who's she?" He looked up, winking at me.

"My ex-fiancée. Apparently, her boyfriend is a muscle head and got hooked on drugged energy drinks and protein bars at his gym." I tried not to sound bitter.

"She could've stayed with you," my newly appointed watch wolf stated flatly.

"That thought had occurred to me." Had her boyfriend been tortured, as well, or turned psychotic by now? Her injuries were severe and a human would've died.

Greg cleared his place at the table. "I don't mean any offense, Cim. I know about addiction and I'd bet this guy has used drugs before. You don't feel different and not notice, especially a gym rat. They know how much their shits weigh."

That visual would keep for longer than I wanted. "It's not any of my business, Greg. She's resting from the ordeal and will fly back to Vegas tonight. It was a call for help, not a romantic visit."

"Two dragons. I wonder." George sat at the table. "I imagine you'd need to clear the room."

"Yes, that's an occasional precaution." Not a topic I wanted to discuss. "Do either of you want to get embroiled in this? There's always a possibility Obsidian is involved. The other choice is a vile demon named Kragen whose drug dealing goes back to hemlock and belladonna."

George shivered. "Does Obsidian really think she's a scientist? First injecting humans with demon DNA and now, maybe, drugs?" The last time he'd stood face to face with her, he'd ended up chained in the basement, Greg across the hall.

I felt like a parent to the two men who lived with me. At over seven-hundred-years old, I had centuries on both of them. The history they read about in high school books were memories for Wretch and me. "Remember that science started as alchemy, and the Asian countries were far ahead of anyone else in developing medicines, poisons, invasion detection systems, and weapons."

Greg's eyes lit up at the prospect. "I'll go but only if Dale says it's okay to leave you here without protection."

Dale had replaced Adam as pack alpha after Obsidian left him in pieces twenty feet from where I stood. He'd assigned him as my bodyguard to keep Wretch's family away from the pack.

"I'm going, as well." My quick exit kept the knowing looks behind my back.

Tanith was on my cell phone when I got upstairs.

"I don't care what your excuse is, you fucking prick! Your buddies from the gym beat me until I had to leave town. If you had anything to do with this, I'll peel your skin off your body."

She hadn't changed. I missed her. "You still have great taste."

Now, I had her boyfriend's number on my phone. That might come in handy.

"Fuck you, Cim. He was a good guy until he got hooked on these new steroids. His muscles grew so fast, I could see a difference every morning."

I closed my eyes. "I really don't want to hear this."

"Don't pretend innocence to me, dragon. You spent a century running around an English village naked to piss off the inquisitors." Her voice held a hint of amusement.

That had been fun. "Can you think of a better way to frighten a misdirected fanatic?"

She laughed. "They tried to hang you how many times?"

"Thirty or forty." Dragon necks didn't snap with human ropes. It would take a steel chain tightened by a demon to kill us that way.

"Well, you should have tried being female and indestructible. I stayed in one noose for a week because I needed a break." Her laughter filled the room.

The dark ages weren't a time for women to do more than smile, nod, and give birth. My repulsion to that oppressive dogma was how I ended up in New Orleans. "You going back to Vegas tonight?"

"Trying to run me off?" She hopped out of my bed, looking like she hadn't been hurt.

"No. The local alpha assigned me a werewolf bodyguard recently and he wants to check out the drug trade in Vegas. We'll stay at Wretch's place while we look around."

I waited for her to start yelling at me. Something about me thinking she needed protecting; how I wasn't capable of doing so; how she used to kick my ass without breaking a sweat—the old favorites.

She stopped short. "You have a bodyguard?"

"Obsidian." That name should explain it all.

"I heard rumors she'd stuck her hand in your face and Wretch threatened to bite it off."

So that's the story told outside of town. "Something a little more dangerous. We killed her human husband, Dr. Brun, Nitha's husband, Narran, and their three kids. Obsidian killed Laythe, the local alpha, and the police chief, both wolves." A shitty week if I'd ever seen any.

"Fuck, Cim. You didn't call in backup?" Her face wrenched in pain and she sat back on the bed. Laythe had been her friend, too.

"We didn't know about the werewolves until she'd signed a two-century self-banishment from the area." I still hadn't been able to read that agreement.

Her laughter twisted from the pain. "You didn't suspect the most devious demon living of pulling one over on you?"

I knew the look on her face even though I stared at the floor. "I'd like to think we saved more than we lost."

"Keep saying that to yourself, Cim. The crusader job you've taken on is more dangerous now with humans multiplying so fast we can't protect them. It was noble during the crusades. Now, it's madness." Humans irritated her.

We'd had this fight so many times; I could recite both of our parts in under ten minutes. "We aren't doing this today."

"I am."

"I'm not. Humans gave us indoor plumbing. Let them breed all they want."

"Wretch is coming back at lunch to get me to Vegas. If your wolf wants a tour and safer place to crash than with you two, he can have my spare bedroom. I promise not to touch him." She kept her word when it came to my friends.

Centuries of betrayal taxed our systems so brutal honesty, even if it meant depriving ourselves of fun and pleasure, worked best in the long run.

"I'll talk to his alpha. I don't know his history, but from what he said, there's a chance addiction is in his past. I'm sure Dale did a full background of his family when he took over the pack." I hoped it amounted to a teenage drinking binge.

"I'm better, by the way, and thank you."

I paused to savor the moment. Missing her took up a section of my heart. "I've told you my doors—all my doors—are open to you until I die. I meant it." I walked away before the memory of her tearing my scales off ruined the moment.

An official Arcane Court letter from Lucan sat on the kitchen table. The eldest living male dragon was the second highest-ranking member of the Arcane Court. It said Obsidian had been removed from her position on the Court. That was a start.

Unfortunately, there was no way the Demon Lords would take her on even without the Court appointment. Lucan apologized for not killing her before she returned to her home in Thailand. Her replacement was Kragen. He hated Obsidian. Not going to help us any, though. The world's oldest drug lord was now a fully sanctioned member of the Arcane Court.

"Fucking fantastic."

"What?" Wretch walked in, smelling like too much cologne.

"The Court replaced your grandmother with Kragen. Tone the smell down. That's awful." I held my hand over my nose.

He shrugged. "Angie likes it."

His nonchalance bothered me. "Drugs kill humans, breaking the Court's own laws."

He shook his head. "No demon forces a human to take the drugs. The drugs kill them; demons don't. It's a devious loophole."

Large enough to keep Kragen out of trouble with the Court. "This can't be good."

"He hates my family."

"He's hated them for millennia and they're still alive. What's wrong? Is he snorting his ambition up his nose?" He'd been around too long to be an addict himself. I could hope, though.

"Quite possibly." Wretch fiddled with his collar.

His nervous twitch worried me. "What?"

"Nothing." Innocence didn't look right on his face. In fact, it faded to sneers within seconds.

I pointed to his hands.

He dropped them. "Kragen can send minions here."

I wasn't concerned. "He's always been able to do that."

"Laythe's team would've slaughtered them the second they appeared."

Then I understood. "Fuck. Now we have to deal with a demon drug lord." Who was distributing drugs manufactured to give powers to shifters and make humans think they were hallucinating. Did it get any more outstanding?

Chapter Three

I didn't know Kragen's end game, or if he even had one beyond the drug trade, but we had to try and stop him. The Dragon Lord in Vegas was a friend, still…to pop in like this might anger Kellen. I hoped we could resolve this with a call. "I have to make a call."

Wretch grunted, smelling the breakfast odors lingering in the air. As I made my way under the archway that separated the kitchen from the front of the mansion, I heard pots rattling.

Wretch could be a chef at any restaurant in the world. He was close to thirteen-hundred-years old, my best guess, and loved it. His dragon and demon combined senses allowed him to smell spices and fragrances I couldn't pick out. Neither could Adam, which led to some fun with the late werewolf.

Fuck, I couldn't get a week between demon lord problems. If Kragen made me miss sparring with Nitha, I'd rip his head off and hang it in place of the chandelier over my head. That made me laugh.

The front doors opened, allowing in a breeze to let me know my neighbors mowed their lawns early today. The southern plantation front porch swing barely held my weight.

I dialed my friend.

"What is going on? I got the message from Lucan so what happened? And where is Tanith?"

He wore his emotions on his sleeve. Good thing his fighting skills proved superb.

"Good morning, Kellen."

"Cim, what's going on?"

"She's here. Her boyfriend went missing. Something about drugs at the local gym."

He snorted; I assumed to keep from laughing. "He's a good guy, Cim."

"Stop it."

"Don't kill him."

That got my attention. "For what?"

"For getting involved in this. He wouldn't do anything to put Tanith in danger. He worships her. It's a little nauseating." He spoke it all in one breath.

I'll say. "We're coming. I'm sure Kragen has a distribution warehouse in his favorite city. It needs to burn down or blow up."

"Agreed. I'll talk to the concierge and make sure Wretch's rooms are spotless and stocked with fresh food."

Kellen's assignment in Vegas included living in City Center.

My partner owned a Sky Villa in Aria. He never told me how he pulled that off; only that it was a very expensive investment—a two-story penthouse with enough room for me to fly.

A short walk around the block should give Tanith time to leave my house. It surprised me I didn't want to spend more time with her. Knowing she'd been safe, under Kellen's and Wretch's watch, eased a lot of my fears. I wish they had told me but we all knew I'd have flown to Vegas instead of moving on. Well, at least physically. The emotional part kicked in when I heard her talk lovingly about her human boyfriend. That proved a blow to my ego. Replaced by a gym rat with a steroid problem. My mother would be so proud.

I called her.

"*Hola* Mama, *como estas*?" If I greeted her in English, she'd yell at me in Gaelic.

"Hi, baby boy. It's been a few days; do you need something?"

"Tanith showed up today."

"Bitch."

"Mother."

"She tried to kill you. Be grateful she's still alive."

I was. "There's a drug ring out of Vegas. Probably Kragen; could be Obsidian. Tanith's boyfriend, human boyfriend, is hooked."

"Whew, boy," my father piped in.

I hated speakerphone. "I'm okay. We're heading over there to eliminate a warehouse. Kragen's been appointed to Obsidian's seat on the Court. Stay out of Vegas for a while? This new drug allows shifters to see demons as they appear, before they're fully back, and humans see demons and shifters but think they're hallucinating."

"We could eliminate demons with this drug, son." My father, the practical warrior. "Could you get us some?"

Did he just ask me to steal drugs for him?

"We're blowing up the warehouse, Dad. I'm sure there is more around. They've hidden it in protein bars and energy drinks sold in gyms."

"Love you, gotta go." My mother hung up.

My parents would get a hold of the drug allowing dragons to see demons, and use it to dwindle the evil demon population. Nitha, Obsidian, and even Kragen could be killed during the few moments they were vulnerable. I preferred that to another round of fighting, rogue demons being more fun to fight; slower, usually intoxicated, and angry.

I waved at the ladies across the street as I turned down the sidewalk to stroll through the neighborhood. They'd called the police once or twice when George and I had wrestled in the front yard. He'd needed to learn how to fight demons and the lessons wandered from the back of the house. The older ladies thought my body slamming him into the ground seven or eight times constituted a beating.

The werewolf officer who arrived explained we were undercover and needed to practice. Now, they sat on their porches waiting for us to take off our shirts. The ninety-year-old gal had a wolf whistle werewolves could hear blocks away.

I kept my shirt on, hearing a huff of disappointment behind me. *Later, ladies; another woman needs to be exorcised from my heart.* Dammit, I wished I'd moved on before she came back. A century wasn't a long time to dragons but still…a hundred years without a partner? I'd been with thousands of women. No one replaced Tanith. My walk became a stomp, my footsteps cracking concrete as I turned the corner, ignoring the protest sounds of the sidewalk.

"Fuck."

"No."

Did my imagination shoot me down? Out loud? Nope, I recognized demon stench.

A low voice behind me grumbled. "You filthy creature."

Turning around, I expected a large man. Instead, I had to look down at a demon possessing a twelve-year-old boy. The child's body wasn't going to survive the day, given the decaying odor. I'd make sure the demon didn't, either. Ripping his head off right there wasn't an option, though.

"I'm betting you won't beat a child in public." His smile revealed braces. Damn, this kid's face was on a poster nearby, I knew it. Those possessions angered me the most. Possessing a child broke Arcane laws and most demons avoided it. No matter how horrific they were to the rest of the world, they'd been parents at some point in their long history. Kids were off limits between dragons and demons. We could leave eggs in the open without worry.

I knew the area we were in well. Wretch and I took a surveillance walk right after Mardi Gras. We needed to know who belonged and who didn't. Greg became familiar as a member of the local wolf pack.

Wretch spent yesterday mounting security cameras on my neighbors' roofs. They wouldn't notice; he'd made them small enough to hide under awnings. The house to our right was the empty one that backed up to my place. If I could lure him into that backyard, I'd kill him instantly.

Then, I smelled his backup.

"Sir, if you continue to harass our son, we'll call the police!" It was shouted loud enough to rouse suspicion but no alarms went up.

The 'boy' walked past me to join the other demons. These had kept their original bodies.

"Do you plan on fucking my reputation with the neighbors?" I stretched my right hand out, extending my dragon claws.

The male growled, glaring at me with yellow eyes. "They already suspect you."

"I'm guessing you're new here. You haven't experienced southern hospitality." All of us attended a neighborhood barbecue and shrimp boil two days ago. One thing we learned—all of our new neighbors were well armed. Seems having demons running about for the past two hundred years led to rumors of night time abductions and missing children. Laythe stopped that when she moved in, but those kinds of rumors, backed up by newspaper clippings now available on the Internet, didn't die.

My scales keep bullets out and Wretch could survive anything that didn't decapitate him, same as all demons. The neighbors didn't know it allowed us to murder anyone they shoot and no one will question the disappearance. It proved a handy arrangement.

"My neighbors will shoot you if you threaten me."

"We'll heal," they said in unison.

"Not in public, you won't. If you shift, they'll get bigger guns and shoot you until nothing is left."

The male reached out and all four of us appeared in the empty home's back yard, with three more demons next to a covered pool.

A while since I'd drowned a demon. I wasn't sure the older ones could walk out before they died, but I was going to enjoy watching them try. Demons' thicker bones and denser muscle structure made them sink. It's why my office and warehouse were by the Mississippi River—easy demon disposal being a real estate requirement.

Around me, the six fanned out. Seemed I was more popular lately. Killing Narran and his three demon children had bolstered my reputation. Most experienced demons pulled farther away. Younger ones, less than a century or two, took it as a challenge.

"Nitha sends her regards," the only female demon said.

I had to laugh. "The demon guarded by her own kind?" I loved the image that painted in my mind.

The largest demon growled at me. "She's more powerful than you."

"I've never denied that. However, you do know you're bigger than she is, right?" It looked like all of his growth spurts went to muscles.

He shook his head. It sounded like a pea rattling around in a plastic cup. He shifted into a professional wrestler outfit.

"Tights are not your best look." I kept my eyes on his face and away from the awkward bulge in his pants. He'd been watching porn.

Wretch laughed next to me. "I wasn't invited?"

George stood next to him, flexing his arms. As a lowland gorilla shifter, he could body-slam a demon into a brick wall. An impressive move. I wondered if he could slam one into the bottom of a pool.

Greg's wolf growl preceded his leap over the back hedge. Landing between two of the demons, he began to pace. The demons near him appeared startled by his size.

Shifting to dragon form, I extended my claws further. The bait boy next to me flinched. Ah, he'd never seen a dragon before. *Playtime.* Grabbing him by the throat, I lifted him into the air.

"You scaly monster."

Smart, too. "Go ahead. Shift."

He couldn't. Even with a demon soul. The boy's body would shred on the first try. The only thing that kept me from dismembering him was knowing the soul of the young boy remained inside, watching. The terror he felt gave the demon a thrill. One I would end in a moment.

"Stop playing with your food," Wretch grumbled, shifting into his favorite demon form—a cross between a room-sized, flesh-colored bat and a vampire. Tufts of hair stuck out at odd angles.

I asked once if this was his natural state. He'd never answered and I let it drop. Must explain his lust for beauty.

My arm shook with pathetic escape attempts. The body would rot faster with the struggle. He had to hold onto the spine and skull to remain there. Otherwise, he'd vanish into the ether. This child's body wouldn't last the day without my intervention.

I removed his head with one swipe of my claws. No one deserved that. The boy's soul escaped with a happy sigh, disappearing into the air.

The demon, however, screeched like a spoiled hatchling. Hissing, ranting, and gurgling sounds accompanied the normal stench. Wretch shifted his talons into blades on the other side of me, slicing the body in half.

"We haven't had a good fight in what? Seventy-two hours?"

His grin split his head in half. Even I cringed.

Greg's barking growl got the attention of the largest demon. I shot a look at Wretch. We knew the wolf would win. He wouldn't be living in my house if he couldn't take down demons on his own.

Greg, along with George, had been injected with demon DNA as a teen. Already a werewolf, it increased his size and strength. George, a human linebacker, became a gorilla. I'd thank Obsidian for their changes right before I tore her head off.

The large demon shifted into a dragon form, bowing to me while keeping an eye on Greg. Even in wolf form, it looked obvious he laughed. The demon hesitated. Greg leapt on the demon's back with his massive jaws locked around his neck. The others came after the rest of us.

We were ready. Wretch, George, and I eyed the remaining four demons. One, who'd played the father out front, and likely the leader, approached George.

One jumped at my head with its arms outstretched. I rocked back to my right leg, cocking my arm back. He slammed into my scales. I thrust my arm through his body, hearing bones crack and organs squish. Finding his spine, I held on, enjoying his panicked shifts.

"Problem?" Cocking an eyebrow, I stared at him until he fell still.

He shifted a dozen times in less than a minute. Both George and the demon he fought paused.

"My turn," Wretch said, shifting to demon form with dragon scales. "If you can't beat a dragon, I'm out of your talent pool," he taunted, jumping into the air followed by two demons.

We didn't need this going public. Two demons and Wretch in the air over a backyard would make the news, even in New Orleans.

The largest managed to pull his oozing neck from Greg's jaws. The werewolf leapt on top of him, gnawing at his skull—only a small difference between the size of his head and Greg's bite.

"Let go of me, you vile lizard," the squirming demon in my hand spat out.

"I've never heard that insult." My sarcasm missed completely. I decapitated him.

He fell to the ground in ashes, a grumpy, green soul left hanging in the air. I let it go, not needing the power-up today. I'd shifted with a tail so when Wretch smacked a demon into the ground next to me, I slammed his head with it. He wobbled to a standing position with a collapsed skull.

The pool cover came off in one swipe. A small shove moved the demon to the edge. I wanted to watch him gasp his last breath. George slammed his demon into the ground with a thud, twisting the head off. I pushed the stunned one in the pool. He gasped for air.

Greg laughed, shifting to human. His demon now towered over him. The inflated ego filled the space as he looked down on a naked man.

"I'll rip your head off," the demon said, pushing his sleeves up.

"Fuck you," Greg replied, kicking the center of the demon's chest.

It knocked foul air out of his mouth in a cloud of odor, giving the werewolf enough time to flip the demon onto his back.

"I take your head," he said as he twisted the neck, yanking the head off.

Damn, he was as strong as Wretch and I. Most werewolves, per Adam, the now-deceased alpha, could snap a neck with wolf jaws, but not pull demons' heads clean off.

"Son of a bitch." Wretch flew over my head. He needed help.

I took off after the demon flying to my back yard. "Wretch, I left one in the pool to play with later."

"Oh, wet demon guts. I'm on it!" He laughed.

I landed in my back yard, grabbing the escapee by the arm.

He turned around, seeing me up close for the first time. "Death Dealer?"

My ego stumbled. "What the fuck? You didn't know?"

Wretch's laughter filtered through the shrubs. "He's faking it, Cim. All demons know you."

"Shut up," I barked, addressing the now-pale demon in front of me. "I'm going to remove your head and drink your soul."

"Uh. No." He blinked.

"Really?" I'm rarely stunned.

Overhead, Wretch flew into the air with a dazed demon in his scaled dragon claws. Right above the pool, he ripped it in two.

"Can I play?" George growled, shifting into gorilla form as he broke through the bushes.

The demon in front of me froze. "You have a fucking gorilla."

"Did you miss the last thirty minutes?" This was a real idiot.

George leapt, crashing the demon to the ground. He put his arms on the deflating chest planted in the grass a good six inches.

"I'm not growing demons in the backyard." The whole lawn would die.

"You pull his head off." George reared back, pacing on all fours.

"We need a door in the bushes," I said, prying the demon from my grass. "You're going to fuel my next fight."

His head came off with a pop; even his soul had lost its fight. Sucking it down didn't give me the satisfaction of listening to screams.

"You would think this would get old." Wretch landed, shifting into demon dandy.

"Never." We lived for these fights. It had become part of our nature. If we didn't have stupid demons to fight on a weekly basis, we'd get bored.

The new werewolf alpha and I needed an alliance, even if he did blame Wretch for the mayhem last week. "I'm going to Dale's."

Wretch coughed. "Tell him I'm sorry. My family is evil."

"They did want you aborted." His parents had been slaughtered after his birth by his aunt Nitha and grandmother Obsidian. His dual dragon and demon heritage made him an abomination in their eyes.

"And keep attempting to do so, over a thousand years later," he said under his breath, going up the stairs.

George bounded next to me in an instant. "He's over a thousand years old?"

"My best guess is plus two-to-three hundred years." I'd never asked him his age.

"That's a long time to run from family."

"Laythe protected him well until four hundred years ago. Something snapped in Nitha and she decided to murder him whenever she could find him. He doesn't talk about the years before that." Only once did he mention living peacefully in the European countryside.

We couldn't fix that family so we needed to concentrate on our immediate problem. "We have a drug dealer problem. I'll fill you in after I see if Dale has any information. Keep an eye out at the bar. This drug affects shifters and humans who take it, makes them see demons."

"That would be one hell of a trip," he said, laughing.

"Which is why we have to blow up every factory. Humans would find us. Do you know what they do to species they don't like?"

"Extinction."

"Yes."

It sounded like he stopped breathing for a moment. *Good. He understood.*

Chapter Four

This was my first time back at the alpha's house since Adam died. Even though he and I worked together for years, I'd stayed away out of respect for Dale. Adam told me it took him months to establish his position. That was before a challenge came to his status, resulting in a cleansing. Adam's stable position as alpha gave New Orleans' paranormals a sense of security. He and his wolves patrolled the streets, keeping all shifters in check. Demons knew stepping over the line with a shifter would alert the wolves who would hunt them down. My job became easier because the pack stayed involved.

"Cim, how are you? Thanks for coming to my father's service." Adam's son met me in the front yard. "I'll let Dale know you're here."

"How are you?" I asked.

"Better. My father said you couldn't pick your family; they're born to you. He made sure I understood Wretch used his abilities to protect others, not kill them. Tell him that for me?"

This kid would be a great alpha one day. "I will."

"Get inside, pup," Dale said, smiling. "'Afternoon, Cim."

Dale stood close to six feet tall with dark blond hair, blue eyes, and a physique that screamed steroids.

The weight of losing two members of the pack, including the alpha, pushed my shoulders down.

Dale stood tall, looking me in the eye. "We did a full records' check, ran background on Obsidian, and found that she's one of the deadliest demons. Her damage to your network and our pack, while painful, was less than she'd done to many of her enemies. We are mourning our losses. I can say unequivocally, you have our help any time you need it."

I blinked. What I wanted to hear but would never have asked. Seemed Adam's pack brought their new alpha up to date on the local demon presence.

"Which brings me to my visit today. An old friend of mine showed up earlier, beaten, and unable to shift due to drugs on the whip. Looks like there's a large drug trade in Vegas tied to the gym industry; protein bars and energy drinks. Greg offered to check it out."

He cocked his head. "With his past?"

"You've hit on my second question. He alluded to a history with addiction. I don't want details but assurances that if he heads over there to check it out, he won't get hooked and put us in danger."

He inhaled. "Your friend female and dragon?"

"Your sense of smell is better than Adam's."

"I'd be dead without it." He smiled. "I'm not going to ask about the overwhelming demon stench. I'll assume they're no longer an issue."

I smelled the wolf part of him. Stronger than Greg's. This was a powerful man.

He continued. "I think he'd be fine. During his teen years, the injections made him an outcast, even in the local pack. He drank often and until he blacked out. Sometimes waking up naked next to dead, skinned, woodland creatures."

"Scary stuff for a teen." I'd done some experimenting with organic compounds in the Yucatan growing up. Hallucinating while flying is an experience I'll never repeat.

"Working with you and Wretch is the most stable he's ever been. If he has you two, he'll stay away from trouble." He sounded sure and nothing in his posture or tone gave away doubts he wasn't verbalizing.

"If we didn't get ourselves caught up in trouble on a regular basis, that would be comforting."

"Our research said Wretch is the next most powerful demon after Obsidian. Do you know who's listed in the top ten and rising every week?" His eyes lit up.

"Nitha has to be in there somewhere."

"She's currently number five, behind Vex and Kragen. You're number ten, Cim. Your absorption of demon magic, especially since you don't burn through it, moves you up faster."

"I'm on a list? That can't be good."

"We compiled it based on very good statistics and centuries of data. I'll send it to you, if you want."

Werewolves loved numbers. They made fabulous accountants.

"I'm good. Wretch will want it." He'd plaster it to his wall and make sure he stayed above me.

"I'll send it over this afternoon. Greg is cleared to do whatever you need him to do. Now that we know your place on the power list, he's safer with you than us."

"That's comforting." I cringed.

"It should be," he said without any irony.

"You understand my reluctance."

"Yes, I do," he stated.

He stood the same height as Adam, with broader shoulders and a more mellow appearance. One look into his eyes, though, and you knew backing away from him amounted to a survival plan.

"Any other research the pack completed I should know about?" I'd grown curious.

"Nothing you should know about," Dale said, smiling.

Wretch would hack into their network. "Thank you. I'll keep you updated about what we find."

The walk back turned quiet. Obsidian left town after she signed the contract. The local demon population plummeted either because she wasn't around anymore, or because Laythe's death removed their positions here. Two days ago, they'd started to trickle back, only different. I needed to find out at the poker game.

The bars along Bourbon Street smelled of human sweat, alcohol, and demons. Puddles littered the streets but it hadn't rained in a month. I wandered between the aromatic post-party leavings and started for Jackson Square. Wretch and I needed to discuss the fate of the warehouse office. Obsidian and the local strays knew its location and that compromised our ability to work there. Seemed we didn't have a location free of demons.

Then again, with an established business front for our Arcane Court work, we could divert the oddest characters from the club.

I dialed his cell phone and he picked up on the first ring. "What are we doing with the warehouse office?"

"I've got workers coming by this evening to clear it out. I negotiated Dr. Brun's space next door, as well. That area holds crates I want to rip into before we do anything else." He sounded like a child with presents to open.

"Furnish them with whatever you want. We can even have business cards." We would keep our fights to the riverside and out of the suburbs.

I could see him in my mind's eye. A businessman with money and a new office to decorate and advertise, he'd stay out of trouble for an entire week. If we didn't have to run to Vegas.

"You know I get all happy when I get to order new business cards and letterhead." He laughed.

"I live to please the demon in you."

"How'd it go?"

"Dale said Greg won't have a problem with drugs in Vegas. You still have a sky suite?"

"Yeah, I own three places there, and one of them contains your ex-fiancée. Or did you think I'd let her live anywhere else?" He dared me to criticize him.

I wasn't surprised to hear he was her benefactor. In fact, that's how I'd met her.

"I have crates to open," he said, hanging up.

Crossing the square gave me a view of the fountain. Tourists stood in small patches, taking pictures of the surrounding buildings and St. Peter's. Our private club sat a short walk away. The front door was closed but I could see Grace and George arguing through the front windows. One corner lay sheltered by brick; it held a card table, or a good demon fight, out of sight.

Worry plagued me until I saw her pick up a fabric swatch. We needed to re-cover the chairs in fabric. Demon smell combined with leather nauseated my jaguar-shifting manager.

The door lock popped when I pushed my key in and the scents of coffee, croissants, and herbal tea filled my nostrils. I blocked out the argument up front— Grace would win—and made my way to the office on the second floor. The mail sat on my river-view desk, opened and sorted. Since I'd hired her, she'd run the office better than Wretch and I combined. My partner won't let the management title go, though; his ego won't allow it. Over the years, he'd taught some of his financial finesse to her.

"That woman is going to kill me." George came up the stairs. "What shifter is going to sit on microfiber?"

"You lost the argument before it started. Walk away and you'll keep more of your dignity," I suggested.

"You win," he said.

"I cheat." I smiled. "There has to be some advantage to being the boss."

He laughed. In the short time I'd known him, I'd come to trust the gorilla shifter. His ability to body-slam a centuries old demon and stick him in a concrete wall helped.

"Of course you cheat." He paced the floor. The room shook. "What is it?"

"Is there something about Grace you're not telling me?" His voice strained.

"Is there a problem *I* need to know about?"

"I'm not sure. She's not herself. Slamming down the phone, taking off for long breaks and leaving the club. Is this normal or…"

"No. I'll ask." Shutting him down confirmed his suspicions. Not like Grace, but I trusted her. She may be sneaking out to spend time with Angie.

"Thank you," he said before heading back downstairs.

I could hear the evening crowd coming in. Things had been lively in our club last night. It seemed a new Demon Lord got appointed to Laythe's position. Neither Wretch nor I knew who it was, and this had us worried.

"Luke called. He's the new Demon Lord," Grace yelled up the stairs.

Pushy demons don't last long. What kind of name is Luke for a demon? "Did you get his number?"

"It's on a pad in the kitchen."

A twitch settled in my back. The demon council had appointed him within hours of Laythe's death. None of the normal two-week period for the infighting, battles, and assignations that typically followed an open demon lord position. Wretch assured me yesterday our reputation changed the process. I doubted it. My suspicions ran to Obsidian appointing her successor and daring anyone to argue.

A thud from the other office pulled my attention from staring at the warehouse across the French Quarter Market. The center of our building was open to the sky, wrapped in glass on every level. We had a small café table and chairs on the ground floor. From my office, I could see across the atrium to Wretch's desk at the back of the building. Leathery pale wings, dark, coarse tufts of hair, and a raptor-like claw dangled a partial body over the floor.

"I don't know what that smell is, but tell Uncle Fester he can't bring that into my bar," Grace said, coming up the stairs two at a time. "Holy shit. Boss, who did you shred?"

I walked to the hallway, running around the atrium, and entered Wretch's office behind her. The odor of decay and rot made me hold my breath.

"Wretch?"

"I've been going through crates, Cim." He shifted back to human form. "Look what I found."

"I'll look at it when my eyes stop watering from the stench. Get that thing outside!"

He vanished with his prize and I heard him shuffling around on the roof.

"He's going to attract every vulture in Louisiana." Grace held her hand over her nose. "I'll get the serious funk spray. You get him to take it away."

I nodded at her and made my way to the stairs. My old bedroom, now occupied by Grace, sat on the third floor with a doorway to the roof stairs. I found a bottle of my old cologne in the bathroom and soaked a towel in it before going up.

"You look like a mugger. Take that thing off your face," Wretch said, grinning.

"No. You to tell me why you brought home half a corpse?"

"I thought you'd never ask. It's Dr. Brun." He had the balls to look proud of himself.

"You killed him."

"And he's still in the warehouse."

"Not all of him."

"Funny, Cim. I mean, Obsidian didn't take his body."

"That's not a surprise, Wretch. She didn't want to touch him when he was alive."

"He smelled nasty, then, too."

I rolled my eyes. "Why?"

"Why what?"

I waited.

"Oh! His body has to be riddled with the drugs he gave Greg and George. Remember them saying he didn't age?"

"Yes, and why do we need his partial, rotting corpse?"

"Angie needs it. She can figure out exactly what changes he made and be able to enter those into her database. Then we can test any demon we want. As long as we get a piece of them, which we always do."

"If you think I'm going to carry specimen bags to poker games, you're wrong."

He was way too happy about this. "Cim, do you think they are the only two successes? No way. There might be hundreds out there, some willing and some unwilling. How many werewolves would love to up the size and power of their pack?"

The scope would be international. Obsidian's home base was in Asia. "You can't appear at Angie's house with this and I don't want it in her secret lab, either." Since that was in my basement.

"That's why I stopped along the way," he said before dialing on his phone. "Angie, I got Brun's body from the warehouse. Yes, really. No, it's not whole. Can I really do that? You'll be able to test his DNA? No, I like that particular part. Okay."

I raised an eyebrow and he ignored me. Demons had natural magic; they didn't need words or potions. They were walking spells. He shifted back to his ten-foot tall bat with pink translucent skin and odd tufts of hair all over—the form that got him shot the first time he and Angie slept together. She nailed him twice between the eyes before he knew he'd changed during orgasm.

The temperature changed as he held both hands over the corpse. Radiant heat flowed from him and cooked the dead doctor to a medium-well.

"Grandpa, crispy." He shifted back to human.

"You're a sick fuck."

"Yes, I am. At least, I didn't ask for utensils."

"Get that thing off the roof. I'll head over to the warehouse. Do I need disinfectant in our space?"

"Nope. I pulled this out of the dumpster a mile away." He vanished.

I assumed to Angie's secret lab in the basement of my place. We needed a coroner and DNA expert to help us track the changes Obsidian and Brun had made. We'd have the first full database of paranormals. The Arcane Court proved wary at first, but when Angie sent the results from George and Greg, they signed on with their full support, genetic engineering seen as a human frailty.

The horrendous odor lingered even through my towel. Back inside, the air had grown foggy. It looked like Grace had emptied every can of Lysol in the building. Her supersensitive smell must've been assaulted.

She appeared through the mist as I got to the second floor with a surgical mask over her face and two cans of orange essence spray on full blast.

"This isn't a plague," I said.

"I wasn't alive then, dragon. It smells like rotten meat and no one is going to buy the bread I made today if it smells like dead flesh." She sprayed me.

"Actually—"

"Don't tell me. Just no." She put her hand up in my face and went back downstairs.

Back in my office, George stood in the farthest corner trying to find any remnant of clean air. I walked around him, opening the balcony doors.

"It would've been nice to know about that an hour ago." He took a deep breath stepping outside.

"I didn't realize Grace would fumigate the place with every spray can in the building," I said, trying not to laugh.

A rattling of the balcony happened as the large man laughed, taking huge, deep breaths. "I've taken gorilla craps that smelled better."

"Okay, time to go." I went to the first floor. "Grace, I'm heading to the warehouse. George will be down when he feels he can walk through the offices."

Once across the street, I turned to see Grace pulling George back inside. The market was full of tourists and locals. A small group of demons grifted around one end. The end of our warehouse building had a sloped concrete boat ramp into the river. I walked around to the water's side, listening as I made my way to the door.

Chapter Five

The door stood open and I heard boxes being moved. Standing on the river side of the building kept me from the crowds, but I couldn't shift in full view. I slipped inside the door, seeing a box move in the back corner.

"Son of a bitch, what do dragons store that's so heavy?" Greg asked, walking around the front.

"I'm not sure what is in that box. It's centuries old and doesn't look like it's been opened." Wretch's past had secrets I didn't know about. I wouldn't volunteer to go through his storage.

"Oh, hello, Cim. Sorry to get started without you."

"You might want to wait until both Wretch and I are here before you open anything." I didn't remember most of what sat in there.

"He said the same thing."

Greg had settled into our group with ease, the restless look in his eyes replaced by a growing confidence. I still wasn't sure placing him firmly in my life had been the best decision for the wolf pack. He amused Wretch. I appreciated his tenacity and fighting skills, so we didn't argue with the assignment. His growth as a fighter would be more necessary now, and any personal issues would need to be brushed aside quickly if he wanted to survive.

"That's because I'm smart and Cim takes after me." Wretch walked through the door, naked.

"Did you forget your clothes when you shifted, or are there some happy young tourists on a boat outside?" I asked.

He looked down. "Both." He smiled.

He didn't smell of rotten flesh. "What did you do with your toasty grandfather?"

"Angie found some uncooked bone parts in there with marrow so she can test him. Just for the record, she appreciated the cooking." He spelled jeans and a t-shirt.

I really wanted to shower now. "I'm sure she did. Grace, George, and I would've liked you to cook him before you stunk up the club."

"Guys?" Greg stood in the open doorway of a crate.

Dust circled his head and I smelled stale mothballs. I never packed with them but Wretch did.

"Look, my old weapons cabinet," he said, walking inside.

Greg looked surprised. "There are hundreds of swords and daggers in here. You can shift into anything you want. What do you need with weapons?"

Wretch moved quickly to find his entire blade collection intact. "There were times when I had to follow strict customs to blend in with different populations. Shifting helps me only if I'm not outnumbered. Besides, there's a grace and beauty to fighting with a good blade. Just ask Cim. He used to teach sword fighting."

I bowed to the werewolf. "Greg, we have extensive personal histories. Mostly made up of fighting."

"I keep forgetting you're ancient." He tried to take the words back as they left his mouth.

"Aged. I'm well-aged," Wretch protested.

I laughed. "Don't remind him he's millennia old. He likes to think of himself as well-seasoned."

"How would you season a demon?" Greg asked.

"Don't joke like that. We've been cooked before."

Wretch has been set on fire a number of times. His womanizing knowledge came at a price.

"But you have to behead a demon to kill them." Our new friend looked confused.

"Exactly." Wretch coughed, drawing a blade across his neck.

"Oh." Quick learner, this one.

I stepped inside. The collection sat in perfect arrangement—swords on the walls, with daggers and knives in boxes with clear tops. "Why aren't these stored at your house?"

"This place is safer. I had them at home for centuries. I decided I wanted an open bar and pool room. So I moved these items here. I'd almost forgotten about them." Wretch held a sword up to his nose and took a deep breath.

I hoped he'd cleaned them since the last time he'd killed someone. "Do we need to leave you alone?"

"Yes." He was enveloped in a memory.

I took Greg's arm, walking over to the kitchen tucked into the back corner of the warehouse. This end of the building held the kitchen, a small living area, and a bed, as well as a bathroom large enough to hold me in dragon form with my wings spread. The only shower where I could spread out and get hot water between my scales.

After the odorous morning I'd had, a shower sounded good. "Wretch, if I walk over to close the door, will I find a gaggle of young girls waiting for the hot, naked man to come back?"

"I didn't make any promises." His voice said otherwise.

Exasperated, I stalked to the door, relieved to find no one outside. A large yacht floated by with a deck full of well-dressed businessmen. "Your audience is gone."

"They'd seen the entire package. No mystery left." He began pulling items out of storage containers.

We had thirty full containers in here and Greg excelled at lock picking. I didn't know how he'd handle being in Vegas. "I'm looking forward to the trip."

"A few days without a case boring you?" Wretch chided me.

"A little bit." I wanted to eliminate all of our problems as soon as possible. This last round hurt more than I'd say. I wasn't looking forward to more centuries of being on evil demon radar.

"I think we all need to go and have some fun." He shifted into demon form, flexing membrane-like wings.

I thought he did that to intimidate me when we first met. In reality, it was an unconscious reaction when he thought about hunting down his family members. Laythe trained him to shift any time his family was near, with the exception of her, for his own safety. It took him fifteen years to unlearn it. Humans shot holes in his wings.

"George will want to go," I said mostly to myself.

"He's protective of Grace and Angie. If you tell him he needs to keep them safe, he'll stay here," Greg said.

"I know. There's a large part of me that wants to see him shift in the middle of a casino floor," I said, smiling.

"You're a sick man," Wretch teased, shifting back to fully clothed human.

"Better yet, in front of Tanith's muscle-bound boyfriend." It slipped out before I knew it.

"Jealous, much?" Greg asked.

"Yes," Wretch and I said simultaneously.

The werewolf laughed and nodded. "Are we going to be roommates in Vegas, or do we each get a hotel room?"

Wretch had invested in every large American city as it grew. He owned more real estate than the loudmouth with the orange, cotton-candy hair. "I own a few places. We'll be in the Sky Suites. There are three bedrooms and enough of a drop from the second floor balcony that Cim and I can fly, if needed. Tanith lives in the Veer."

"You should apologize to Grace for the stench at the bar before we go," I said, walking to the bathroom. "I need a full wing cleansing."

The area we cordoned off for living space took up a full third of the warehouse. For a demon who grew up in shacks and a dragon from a small Mexican village, space amounted to a luxury and we never let a chance slip by to get more of it.

Which is why Wretch bought real estate and I bought land. I even owned a couple of stars and space on the moon. I was seven-hundred-and-fifty-plus years old and positive humans would be colonizing space before I hit a thousand. Lower gravity intrigued me; how would I fly? How high could I get above the moon before I got pulled back? Could I throw a demon hard enough to launch her into space?

The step-in shower sat seven feet wide and five feet deep. The glass and stone glistened. One yellow light shone from the corner, making it a private, cozy place. I decorated this to resemble the corner quarry my parents and I used to bathe in. Raised in the Yucatan Peninsula among natives, we had very little but the natural views were spectacular.

The smell of clean water mixed with lemon as I took the organic soap Grace gave me for Mardi Gras and rubbed it on my human skin. Muscles rippled as I turned and twisted to clean myself before I shifted.

In dragon form, I spread my wings as far as I could and let the scalding hot water pour over me. My additional six inches of height after absorbing Narran's magic had my head almost at the ceiling. Steam rolled, filling every corner as I let the water cleanse me.

Las Vegas. I hadn't been back since Nitha tried to killed me there ten years ago. Wretch attempted to take me back five years ago but I refused. His ability to appear and disappear at will would allow us to get there instantly. I wanted to prepare mentally for the memories. I'd fought her dozens of times to a standstill, or until Wretch showed up to back me up and she fled. That time, we'd ended up at the rooftop pool above the residences at City Center.

I'd run into her downstairs. Nitha gambled in the poker room down in the Mandarin Hotel. I'd walked in, overly confident, with women following behind me like I was a playboy. My guard had been down as I tried to emulate my best friend's casual sexual prowess. It looked fake on me and didn't fit well. The room went quiet as we entered and the dealer nodded at Nitha.

She rose from her seat, dressed in a skin-tight, red sequined dress—she'd have been pretty if I hadn't known the decay and death hidden behind the façade. At five-foot-tall with brown hair, she blended in with humans, barely noticed most of the time.

"Cimmerian, we need to speak." She grabbed my arm, pulling me out of the back door, and we vanished.

We appeared on top of the building and she dunked me into the pool. I scratched and clawed at her skin. She shifted, the red dress replaced by scales as she took on a reptilian shape. Her clawed hands around my throat, she slammed me against the deck. My hands shifted and I used my three-inch claws to rip open her flesh. She shifted, healing in the process, but never let go of me.

I, too, shifted, but with only dragon and human forms to choose from, she knew what would be appearing in front of her, giving her an advantage. I couldn't shift into a form without a neck and head at the top.

We fought for an hour before I heard Wretch shouting for me. I couldn't answer; each moment, I grew more afraid I wouldn't breathe again. I was able to break both of her arms and shatter her knee, and each time, she healed as I fought for my life underwater.

When Wretch walked out onto the deck, she pulled me into the deep end and held me there. We vanished and appeared in the swamp outside New Orleans. It took me a second to notice the water had changed from chlorinated to filled with life. Alligators swam to us as we struggled. They waited to see who would be left alive. She shoved me down to the bottom. I held what little breath I had left as she ripped the scales on my chest. I twisted her head until her neck snapped; I felt the cracking of her spine. Without any breath left, I hoped she drowned since I couldn't remove her head.

I don't remember anything else until two days later when I heard Laythe and Wretch discussing who to call to repair my broken, drowned body. I drifted in and out of consciousness, for what Wretch later told me was weeks, as they worked to repair my system.

My ability to absorb demon magic saved my life as they killed five nasty thugs and let me drink their souls. That's when Laythe and Wretch told me I was becoming a demon. No other answer as to how I healed and shifted at demon speed after absorbing souls. Each time I absorbed another soul, my skills and senses improved. This last time, with Narran's soul, I grew six inches in dragon form and my sense of smell doubled.

Nitha survived, as well, gone by the time Laythe and Wretch found me. The demon council removed her magic. Her family stood by while other demons absorbed her powers. They became psychotic and suicidal within weeks. Laythe had them killed quietly one night, with Wretch there to make sure their souls didn't find another host.

The Arcane Court forced me to take ten years off. To immortals, that wasn't a long time. I hadn't had a vacation in four hundred years. I wandered around, traveled to Europe, and spent time with my family in the Yucatan. My parents travelled every other month and loved to go on cruise ships. They could fly but choose to sit on a slow-moving boat.

The number of souls I absorbed along the way increased my magic abilities tenfold. Killing rapist demons in London, drug dealers in South America, and the random bounty hunter hired by Nitha kept me sharp. Wretch taught me how to spell clothes for others. The enhanced senses alone were worth it. Like my new height. I could see demons as they appeared near me, but only in dragon form.

Demons backed off while I was gone, Nitha's removal of power the primary reason. They realized the Demon Council would enforce the laws on the books from time to time. Which made knowing when they could fuck up very difficult. It proved amusing. You could see the confusion on demons' faces as they weighed consequences. Wretch got a few on video before he killed them for doing it, anyway.

Nitha sat trapped in a European countryside oubliette surrounded by demons who'd love to kill her if she could get out. Wretch and I would welcome her death even more if someone else did it.

I heard a pounding on the door, unaware of how long I'd been in there. Turning the water off, I shifted into human form and grabbed my robe from the back of the door.

Wretch stood on the coffee table in front of the large flat screen television blaring the Discovery Channel. He loved the Mythbusters.

In front of him on the couch sat Greg, doubled over in laughter. "Do it again." Tears ran down his face.

"I think that's enough for one night." He loved to imitate the crash test dummies on the show. Given his gift for shifting into gross and deformed shapes, he was more accurate.

"I want to play poker with some demons before we leave. If it's an operation run by one of the Lords, they'll know." I wanted the local population to hear me asking questions before we left. Anyone expecting us on the other end would then answer for his or her New Orleans connections.

"Why would they tell you anything?" Greg went to the fridge for a drink.

"With Obsidian self-banished and Nitha under watch, they feel less obligated to watch their words. If our problem is now Kragen, they'll talk. Drug dealers of any species make enemies in their own ranks." I took a cup of tea he'd prepared while I cleaned up.

"I deserve an award for that performance." Wretch jumped down from the table. "It was brilliant."

Young demons, less than a thousand years old, had moved to town recently and I wanted to find out what they knew. Some of them surely came from Vegas. Keeping an eye on Tanith from a closer vantage point would be an added bonus. Kellen, the dragon assigned there, and I had the busiest dragon jobs in the US.

I would miss New Orleans, even for a few days. There thrummed a unique and individual atmosphere in the French Quarter. Not to mention, if I needed to get away quickly, the Gulf of Mexico was minutes away by air. I could fly for ten minutes and land where I couldn't be found.

We both had escape kits packed at all times. Mine sat unopened; Wretch had to use his seventy years ago when one of his sex partners had been the wife of a prominent politician. He took on another human form for a few months until the politician lost his bid for office. I knew Wretch planned the loss. I never asked him about it. A large part of our friendship was complete trust in the other's judgment.

Usually discreet in his amorous affairs, that had been a rare slip-up for him. His latest attempt at an honest relationship was Angie. He loved her, and I was sure she loved him, as well. His life—our lives—didn't make it easy. She was human and, as much as it hurt them, they were better off as lovers and not serious. That made her a target. We thought we'd lost her last week and I'd never seen Wretch so distraught over a woman.

I wanted to talk with Grace and George before we left, too. They needed to keep a low profile with us out of town.

"How many containers did you open?"

"All of them," Greg said. "Your stuff is in the back three."

He gestured to the far corner and I made my way over there. Inside the first one, I found items from my childhood room. It had been small in the Mexican hut so there was little there. A couple pieces of pottery my mother helped me create. They were awful, deformed birds with colors that ran together and looked streaked. I loved them.

"Did that bird get run over by a car?" Greg asked.

"No, I tried pottery for a day. This was the result."

"You're a better killer."

"Yes."

He backed out of the crate. "Hard to believe you and Wretch have been doing this for four hundred years."

"We move around, travel all over the world, even had to run down a demon playing an abominable snowman in Alaska. I'm never bored, always compensated, and rarely outmatched in skill and strength. I have a good life. Besides, we've been settled here for two hundred years. With a huge tourist population, and very little interaction with humans, we can remain here."

"Then I have found my dream job." His smile lit up his eyes.

"If it doesn't kill you."

"I had the option of saying 'no' to Dale after Adam and Mike died. I chose to stay because of the risks, not in spite of them." He sounded angry.

That raised concerns. "You an adrenaline junkie?"

He smiled "Not at all. I even drive slow. My body and mind are built, engineered, for fighting, but I don't look for fights. I end them."

Something in his tone and the way he held his body ready to pounce when he said that made me believe him. This man would be either in trouble or stopping it no matter where he worked. At least with us, we had a chance to keep him alive.

Dr. Brun's screwing around with his DNA may have long-term consequences. Angie tested samples from him and George to find out. Best to keep him underfoot until we knew the answers. That way if, and when, it went bad, we'd be there to clean it up.

We rummaged through the crates, recalling memories. I marked my childhood items so I could put them in a safe deposit box. One way to keep them safe enough to pass down. I didn't have any children, and wasn't planning on it, so at that time, Grace would get my things. Wretch had so many piles of legal paperwork for his estates, I'm not sure he knew who was going to claim it.

Morose thoughts swam through my mind, mixed with childhood memories, as I walked back to the club. The smells of sweaty tourists and powdered sugar greeted me as I passed the west end of the market. Wretch and Greg would organize the rest and appear at my place when they were done.

Chapter Six

"If you still smell like burnt psychotic relative, don't you dare walk in here," Grace said as I stepped into the club.

It smelled like an orange tree had exploded. George stood behind the bar with a surgical mask on his face.

"It wasn't that bad," I said, getting a cup of coffee, lying.

"She's gone a little overboard with the spraying," he answered, cleaning off the bar. "You need to talk to her. Something is wrong."

She hissed at him. "I'm fine, okay. I told you that earlier, ape. Now leave me alone."

"As soon as you hand me my head back," he growled.

Grace looked up at the tone in his voice. "Sorry, George. That was too far."

I followed her back to the kitchen. A door led to the three-story open courtyard. She grabbed a pot of tea from the stove, filling a cup before heading outside for fresh air. She loved this area.

"Explain," I said.

"You don't order me around. Or at least, you never used to."

"This type of behavior is completely unlike you," I started, careful not to get her angry at me. She scratched.

"It's Billy," she said, staring at the ground.

"Who's Billy?"

"My boyfriend."

"I didn't know you had a boyfriend."

"Some detective you are." She smiled.

"I understand why'd you'd keep us a secret from him. You can't keep him a secret from us. Anyone who might be used as a pawn against you should be on a list in my office." I thought of, and treated her, like a daughter.

"What is up with you today? All business and cold?"

I noticed tears running down her face and changed my tone. "What happened, Grace?"

"He disappeared. He was running with a bad group before we met. I know it's only been two months, but I was falling in love with him and then he vanished. He didn't take anything with him." She paused sobbing. "He left pictures of us on his bedside table."

"Was anything missing?" I went into work mode.

"His wallet, a backpack he took when we went bike riding, and all of the sports drink he was selling at the gym."

This was bad. No way we could get to Vegas without Grace if there stood a chance her boyfriend might be there. I debated not telling her there could be a likely link. I didn't know if George talked about Tanith's visit this morning. Fuck. "What brand was it?"

"What?"

Her mind had moved on.

"The sports drink?"

"Red Lady. Guaranteed to make you see things that aren't there and get stronger than any other human." She recited what had to be the tagline.

Of all the stupid assed things to name a drugged drink. "That's on the bottle?"

"Yes, he repeated it every time he drank one of them."

"Is Billy human?"

"No. He's a cat shifter, like me."

I told her about Tanith and her experience with the dealers in Vegas. If I didn't come clean and we found his body in Vegas, she'd leave me. I could handle most other women walking out of my life; not Grace. Or Tanith. Damn, this was a bad day.

"You think he went to Vegas?"

"It appears to be the home base, at least in the US, for this operation. I'm not saying he was planted here, but I wonder if he was paid to get close to you." If it wasn't about us, I'd be surprised and relieved.

She'd been around us long enough not to get offended at my suggestion her man was only with her because of us. "You're going go get him back."

"Yes. Wretch, Greg, and I are going to blow their warehouse up. I know this may be hard for you, but I don't want you there. If Billy isn't in there, we won't go looking for him. He may be bait. This screams demon drug operation and I need you here, listening, and keeping George in line." I paused, waiting for her look at me. "You need to apologize to him. You called him un-evolved."

"He made me so mad. I don't even remember what he said." She sighed. "I'll apologize. Bring Billy back, will you?"

"I just said he may be bait."

"If that's the case, bring me his head."

I truly loved her.

She stood up, shifted into a jaguar, and walked to the door. I opened it and she vanished up to her apartment, formerly mine. I went to the bar to refill my coffee and George stood alone by the bank of windows facing the road. Outside, three demons were pushing a human couple around in the street.

He looked at me, raising an eyebrow. I nodded. He walked outside, glanced up and down the road, grabbed the demons, and carried them to the sidewalk. He waited until the humans ran toward Jackson Square. The demons were new in town and that meant they would push their power around until one of us stepped up.

George stood quietly on the sidewalk under the overhang and waited. The demons bounced around like actors in a hip hop video until they decided to attack. One vanished and appeared next to George on his left, another on his right. The third proved even more stupid and appeared next to me at the door.

I reached out with my right arm, shifted my hand into a claw, and slashed his throat. I didn't decapitate him because I wanted him to see what happened to his friends.

The two demons with George wrapped their arms around him and squeezed. A move that killed humans in minutes. They didn't know George was a shifter.

He stood straight and pulled his arms to him, breaking out of the demons' grip with ease and they stumbled back, surprised. He walked inside, a demon in each hand. Shifting to lowland gorilla, he grasped their necks, picking them up into the air, and slammed them into the floor.

"Holy shit. Where the fuck did that guy come from?" The slowly healing demon next to me asked.

"My bag of tricks."

"You going to kill me now?" It was a request.

"No, heal up and get out. Make sure you tell every pesky demon who wanders into the clubs and poker games that there's a gorilla shifter capable of lodging you in walls, sidewalks, and streets."

I turned to watch his face as he thought about that. A demon stuck in the road overnight would be repeatedly run over, heal, and run over again. I liked that idea the more I thought about it. He obviously didn't as he paled and vanished.

George shifted back to human, dragging the two demons with him. He dropped them on the street. I spoke the spell for clothing for him. My store of demon magic would last me months.

One advantage of being in New Orleans was even when humans posted the picture on their internet accounts, no one would think twice about it. George turned around, blowing a kiss to the tourists across the street.

"You're going to be popular on someone's vacation page," Grace said from behind the bar. "Not exactly undercover."

"They won't remember anything but my ass," he said, smiling.

"Well, I got the front view and now I need a drink," she said, heading for the special liquor cabinet.

Wretch appeared in the private dining area. We'd blocked it off so we could shift without alerting humans outside.

"All of the containers have been opened and catalogued. Greg's very good at organization." He watched Grace cautiously.

She poured two fingers of a three-hundred-year-old scotch and downed it one gulp. "Don't stare at me like that. My boyfriend is missing. You're lucky I don't turn up the entire bottle."

"I've never seen you drink," George said.

"I don't like it."

Wretch laughed. "The only time we got her drunk, a demon came in and tried to fight her. She shifted and barfed a hairball on his shoes."

The look on her face told Wretch he was in trouble. Meanwhile, George and I were laughing so hard, tears ran down our faces.

"It was an accident. I'm not a kitten," she said, looking angry and hurt.

I walked over and wrapped my arms around her. "We know that, Grace. You wouldn't be here if you couldn't handle yourself. We've all done some strange things when exposed to magic or alcohol."

"I shifted on Halloween when I was tending bar and body-slammed the entire band into the back wall of the club," George said. "Most of the guests thought it was a costume but the guys I hit knew better."

"Did they run to the news or internet to talk about seeing a gorilla?" Grace asked.

He looked down at his feet. "No, they told the media I was an angry monkey."

Grace shook with laughter as I held her. We both tried to hold it in. It didn't work. We burst out laughing and held each other up. Wretch, on the other hand, shifted into a howler monkey and danced on the back tables.

Angie came in through the front door in the middle of his display, walked over to him, and grabbed his tail, dragging him to the kitchen. That was a first.

We didn't follow. A few seconds later, I heard, "Take your hand off there, you dirty pig!"

He must've shifted again because she laughed. "I recognize that face. I put four bullets in the forehead."

Wretch returned in human form with his normal casual linen slacks, buttoned-down shirt, undone, shoulder-length dirty blond hair, and blue eyes. Most women swooned over him, and even some straight men.

"Angie found an anomaly in your DNA," he said to George.

The gorilla nodded. "More than Dr. Brun's manipulations?"

"Apparently, we'll need to study it more, but it seems you had a shifter in your family tree."

"What are the odds?" Grace said.

"Quite high," Angie replied, coming in with a drink from the kitchen.

"Most humans have shifter DNA. They're different races but interbreeding did take place quite often in the past. Usually, the children would grow up human with some sensory enhancement. Now, though, since the Court ordered no interbreeding four hundred years ago, the strains are weak," I explained.

"This makes the entire human population a target for Obsidian," Grace noted.

"It's always been her target," Wretch said.

"Your family sucks," she said.

No one replied. It was a fact. I wanted to ask Angie if she'd traced her own DNA. I made a mental note to ask Wretch later.

"I need food," Grace announced, walking back to the kitchen.

Wretch and I followed, leaving George to get details about his DNA. I tried to overhear what shifter was in his past but couldn't do so without being obvious.

The three of us, practiced in the art of cooking around one another, created a large lunch. At the house, George handled food preparation, but here, we did. Steaks, overly large cheeseburgers, bacon, two pounds of fries for the four of us and a chef salad for Angie. Her metabolism couldn't handle large doses of meat without expanding her waistline. Something she'd made us aware of early on, and that our trying to increase it was not a compliment. Human women—I loved their curves, but each one came with her own rules.

Shifters burned through calories so our concern stuck to getting too little food. Back in Mexico and then in England, I would hunt large game two or three times a week and consume it raw or singed over a fire. Doing that in the open field had been a great way to meet other shifters. Then again, I did mistake one large wolf pack for shifters when they weren't. I shifted and they ran from me. It helped to look like a dinosaur.

Angie pulled together two large tables from the bar and we sat down to eat. No one asked me about Tanith and I'd been waiting for more questions. One look at Wretch told me he'd warned them. So I opened up first. This group needed to know some of the history in case things went wrong in Vegas, or this problem followed us back home.

"Tanith and I dated for fifty years before I asked her to marry me. She's the only dragon female I could stand to be in a room with, other than my mother. Dragon women are in high demand for breeding purposes and can name their price. Tanith told every male she wasn't a breeder, and she wanted to have children with a lover, not as part of a business deal."

I heard Grace's and Angie's intakes of breath. They didn't know how small the dragon community was and the six and seven figures a female could make for each child she bore a non-relative.

Tanith had ten siblings, two sisters and eight brothers. Her sisters both offered to bear my children while we dated. I never told her. It's why they still breathed.

"I figured you for the strong, quiet type," Angie said to me, winking at Wretch.

He rolled his eyes. "You don't get out of my bed, my house, and then flirt with my best friend, you minx." He was turned on.

"She's not your wife," Grace stated, starting at me. "Why is that?"

"She left me at the altar." I tried to hide my pain. I spent years trying to be the dragon she wanted. I curbed my appetites, hunted only at night, courted her like the humans, and still, she tried to remove my heart with her claws.

"Tell them more," Wretch said.

A flash of anger crossed his eyes. He was still pissed off. She'd opened up my chest and dug around until she found my heart. Wretch sewed me up, stole blood to help me heal, and sat with me until I healed.

"She didn't show up for the wedding. Later that night, as I slept at the warehouse, she came by and tried to tear my heart out." After being dosed with a drug, I suspected.

Grace looked skittish as she spoke. "Drugged by Obsidian?"

"That's my guess now. Then, there was no explanation. She vanished and I hadn't seen her again until she showed up in my bedroom doorway." Looking gorgeous and wounded. My two favorite things.

My love for her never waned, heart removal attempt included. My suspicions were Nitha was involved and Wretch agreed. Now that we knew the kind of DNA manipulation they could do without harming human anatomy, it wasn't hard to imagine the extent of their knowledge.

Chapter Seven

Time to get ready for Las Vegas. The look on Wretch's face told me he was worried about this trip—both of us outside of New Orleans for the first time since Obsidian signed her agreement. A risk, but I refused to be isolated to one city.

I wanted both Angie and Grace to stay for the safety factor. George would watch over them and, as much as Grace hated it, she needed someone nearby. Her jaguar form kept her at knee level. George could climb concrete walls with her on his back if he needed to get higher up for any reason.

"Grace, keep the garden door open while we're gone." I nodded to George.

"Yes, sir." She sounded pissed. "Any other suggestions, *father?*"

I wanted her safe and if that made her angry, I'd learn to deal with it. "If you start to close it, get angry about any of the suggestions we make, or don't check in with Wretch, remember how Adam and Mike looked in my foyer." Mean of me to remind her of the dismembered werewolves in pools of blood.

It worked. "You play nasty."

"I have to. Greg will be going with us; George will stay here with you. Our contact from the Arcane Court will continue to send messages to us. Don't turn your cell phone off, even to screw someone."

"I'd appreciate a video call when that happens," Wretch said, smiling.

"No way, Uncle Fester. My sex life is not for your sick pleasure," she replied. "I love you two. Don't get killed."

"We, my dear, won't die." He assured her. "If the drug ring is centered in Vegas, you can be sure my grandmother is in her Phuket fortress feigning innocence."

"It's drugs, Wretch. Think Kragen. His henchmen's tactics are all over Tanith's beating and her boyfriend's disappearance." I noticed Angie's confused look. "It's going to be run by minions, lower demons trying to earn his favor. It helps to think of demon society like the mafia you see on television. He's a boss with a huge, ancient organization of demons, shifters, and probably humans, doing the day-to-day chores. Tanith's boyfriend is human. We need to find out where he worked, follow the distribution trucks back to the local factory, and blow it up."

All three steps sounded simple. I expected a lot of complications. It's why I was still alive four centuries after starting my job. Most enforcers for the court got killed in their first century of service. Wretch helped. If my colleagues had had a demon-dragon hybrid by their side, it would've significantly raised their survivability rate.

"I can do that research online," Grace offered. "Unless you want to call her and ask."

"I'll call her," I said, dialing the number Wretch had displayed on his phone.

"I don't know who you are but you damn well better return my boyfriend before I rip your heart out with my bare hands," she screeched.

A headache started behind my forehead. "Sounds like you've healed," I said, holding the phone at arms' length.

Wretch laughed.

"You bastard. Of course, I'm healed."

"Who has your boyfriend?"

"If I knew that, I wouldn't be yelling at every number I don't recognize. How the hell do you do your job?"

Ah, she's back in my life. I needed this reminder as to why she'll never be a romantic interest again. "Wretch and I are coming to town. We will have a werewolf with us, staying in Wretch's penthouse. Text me the name of his gym and his workout schedule."

"I didn't ask for your help." She sighed.

"Showing up in my bedroom bleeding counts as a cry for help. Or don't you remember our last conversation?"

"Fuck you. Arrive safe." She hung up.

Wretch smirked. "She's the only woman who can get you to make that face."

I tried to stop scowling. It took some work. She annoyed me more than anyone else. My father used to say it meant she should be my wife. At one time, I'd agreed.

The day I met her, I'd been fighting demons in New York. The humans had named Hell's Kitchen correctly. I took on four young demons after a street card game went bad. Three of them turned to ash and, as I turned to the fourth, I saw her.

Five-foot-eleven with waist-length red hair and white skin stands out, even at two in the morning. She stood still, waiting for the demon to notice her. It didn't take long since I was transfixed. He followed my gaze and gasped.

Tanith smiled at us and spread her wings. The demon drew back his right hand to grab the knife tucked in his back waistband.

Her first words to us were spoken with a beautiful Scottish accent. "I'll take the demon's head first."

I crossed my arms over my chest and watched her. The demon threw his knife at her and she caught it in mid-air. After twirling it in her hand a few times, she threw it at the concrete and embedded it two inches. That meant power, and I'd wanted her from that moment.

Until this one, if I was honest. No one intrigued me like she did. Then, after a few decades together, the newness wore off and I, stupidly, thought marriage would spice things up. My prowess with women started and ended in the bedroom. A talent I'm proud of, but it doesn't fill every hour.

After the attack, Wretch watched me turn inside on myself with pain as I healed. He never told me what he did; only that if I didn't get better, he would hunt her down. I pretended to be healed.

It took a few years before I had another relationship; even so, I never forgot my Scottish beauty. And now, she's with a human. That didn't feel right. Some things she liked to do in bed, a human couldn't survive. No wonder she hunted for gym rats. *Endurance.* Hell, even in my own head, I sounded bitter. I needed to rein it in before I met the poor bastard.

"How long will it take you to pack?" Angie asked Wretch.

"We don't have to pack. My clothes are of my own making and Cim keeps a closet full of clothes there. We have the ability to appear in my homes all over the world without a thing."

"No wonder you two stay single." She grimaced.

Their break-up had been hard on her. She knew he loved her and that he was over a thousand years old. It hurt her to hear about women he loved before her, or the many ways we had of vanishing in a moment to return years later.

"Women live longer if I vanish," he replied.

Humans lived such short lives. Their prime active and healthy years amounted to less than four decades. Over so fast.

"Greg, let's get back to the house so you can pack. I'll make a last check of the warehouse. Wretch, meet us there in an hour?" I wanted to be there.

"I'll set the security systems up," he said, vanishing.

"We'll be gone for a short while, likely no more than a few days. The Court won't require proof for us to kill anyone involved with this. It will take little time to find Tanith's boyfriend. Then, we'll be back and do most of the investigating of the drug trade from here. Sooner or later, every demon makes the Vegas to New Orleans to New York route, and we're safer here."

Grace hugged me. "Be careful, boss. That bitch can get you out there."

"I promise." Hiding wasn't my style.

George stood silently.

"You take good care of her?"

He nodded. It appeared my gorilla shifter wasn't good at goodbyes. I walked over to the warehouse. The crates stood open with the items pulled forward. Memories rushed back as I saw pottery from Mexico and swords and daggers I'd made in England.

The bedside table looked ancient. I'd re-sanded it a few years ago to look more modern. The false bottom in the drawer held a necklace and ring. Tanith mailed them back to me and Wretch intercepted them. Years later, he gave them back when he thought I'd healed enough.

Standing there holding them, I realized I wanted to be over her. Seeing her with her human boyfriend would arouse jealousy, but I stayed determined to push it aside. My life was good as it was. One day, I might fall in love again, but I wasn't in a rush. I had centuries left to live and planned on enjoying as many women as I could until one reached out with her eyes and stole my breath.

I returned the items to their hiding place. George had a key to this location and I'd instructed him to come over here once a day during our absence to check in.

My hope was to get to Vegas, straighten out the demons who messed up Tanith, kill the local person running the drug operation, and get back home in less than a week.

I needed to remember to find Grace's boyfriend, Billy. Even though I didn't want to. That protective fatherly streak wouldn't let up. Especially since she didn't trust him enough to introduce us. That proved a first, and made me suspicious. I needed accurate intelligence. The door snapped shut and the lock automatically engaged.

The Mississippi River appeared beautiful as it meandered by during my short walk back to the club. Grace and George worked in the front and I found Wretch in his office on the second floor. When I'd handed most of the club operations over to Grace, she'd taken up residence in my office, leaving Wretch his own space. She'd never said anything aloud and I knew she cared for him, but she'd never truly trusted Wretch.

"I'm playing poker tonight. You want to come, or do you plan on sitting in your security cave and staring at screens all night?" He had better security than the American government. He'd never been hacked.

"There are benefits to sitting quietly and observing." He smiled.

"Watching boobs bounce down Bourbon Street doesn't do us much good."

"Yes, it does." He laughed.

"I'll keep my phone on me tonight." He'd bought me the latest, most expensive new toy. The least I could do was take it with me. "Is there a 'spy mode' on that thing so I can sit it on the table and let you listen in?"

"Yes, but they'll know it. Keep it in your pocket on 'vibrate.' I can track you with the GPS signal in case anything happens."

"I will not be running naked down the street again."

"I can hope," he said.

"Pervert."

"Born that way." He started singing Lady Gaga. His voice could curdle milk.

"I can hear that. Stop singing before I want to tear my ears off," Grace yelled from downstairs.

"Cat hearing." He grinned.

"You keep teasing her and she'll claw your eyes out."

"They grow back."

Grunting and screaming from downstairs stopped our discussion. Wretch vanished as I ran down.

George stood behind the bar with a smile on his face. It looked like he hadn't moved. Grace was on the front side of the bar between two tables. A demon, who'd hit on her before, held her up by the neck, pressing her back against the front windows.

She looked bemused. "Nice move, demon. How do you plan on getting my panties off if I don't breathe?"

"I don't need you to breathe. I want your body; you being in it at the time is optional." He smiled and I thought I saw something crawling on his teeth.

Wretch appeared four feet to the demon's right, in the private section, pulled out a chair, and sat down.

"This will be good," he said, putting his feet up on the table.

The demon laughed, and the stench made Grace's eyes water. "Even your friends aren't worried about you. They want to watch me abuse you. I knew this town would be easy since the big bitch abandoned it. I never thought it'd be this easy."

So Obsidian let it out about her leaving New Orleans. That would cause problems if the younger demon population decided they wanted to claim it.

"What makes you think it'll be easy?" I shifted my gaze.

He looked over at me and saw my orange dragon eyes replace the hazel ones.

"You can't threaten me, Cim. The Death Dealer is no more. Obsidian made sure you'd be hunted if you left town and offered millions to anyone who could take out your friends. The prices on your heads will have hundreds of demons here by tonight."

I smelled Greg before I heard his claws clicking on the polished hardwood floor. His wolf head bumped my hip, letting me know he was there.

"Then I think we need to send a message to the incoming horde. Wretch. How many words can we carve into his back before he passes out?"

"I love this game." He stood up.

George hadn't moved but I could hear his breathing get stronger. Greg stood at my right side and Wretch walked halfway to the demon.

Grace folded her arms and crossed her legs. "Do I even need to say it?"

"As long as I have you, they won't touch me," he said.

Stupid demon.

Centuries of fighting and shifting individual body parts allowed Wretch and I to extract anyone from a demon's grasp. Even in fire. I'm fireproof. A handy fucking thing in the years before fire trucks.

My best friend smiled as his right arm grew. He liked taking the shape of octopi and squid. The suckers had needle-sharp points that could pull circles of flesh off a body.

The demon didn't notice. He took his free hand and started to trace his fingers across Grace's cheek. I was proud of her. She flinched but didn't smack him right away. When his fingers trailed down her neck and started for her cleavage, she uncrossed her legs, braced her arms against the window, and kicked him in the shin.

He liked it. "Kick me again, beautiful. I want you to struggle."

She obliged. This time, I heard his kneecap pop. He wobbled for a moment but demon magic and survival skills came as reflex and he healed in moments.

The long arm Wretch stretched out started to wind around his legs, loose enough so he wouldn't feel it. He was too focused on Grace to notice death wrapping around him. Grace waited. The demon placed his hand near her breast, not touching her but teasing. She bit her lip. If we hadn't been there, she'd have shifted by now and shredded him. Her skills didn't include the ability to kill him but she could slow him down. Her jaguar speed allowed her to escape on previous occasions.

"Look down," Wretch said.

The demon saw the arm. He shifted one hand into blades, maintaining his grip on Grace, then started cutting parts of Wretch's arm off. Each time he did, it grew back. Greg sat down and looked up at me. He was my bodyguard and unless I was in danger, we'd told him not to get involved. Glad he'd listened. A fight between demons changed in seconds as their twisted imaginations conjured up weapons.

George brushed past me, handing me a cup of my favorite tea on the way. He walked around to Grace, her neck held tight in the demon's grasp. Without shifting, he took the wrist at her neck in one hand, the elbow in his other, and snapped the arm in two.

Grace screamed as he pulled the now-stiff appendage from her neck. They were covered in blood as they made their way back to the kitchen.

Wretch noticed this, winking at me as they left the room. "Now that they are out of the way, how about we finish this?"

"If this is the best you can do, it's no wonder your family is ashamed of you. The dragon genes made you weak."

Idiot demon.

I heard Greg cough and I wasn't sure if he was surprised or laughing.

My friend let go of the demon, shifting back to human. His hair in perfect place, his shirt unwrinkled, he even cleaned the dark brown linen pants of blood as he changed.

The demon looked over at him like he couldn't believe he'd won. "You gave up? I'm going to enjoy killing you."

Wretch pulled the demon until both were unseen from the front windows. Then he spoke the freezing spell.

"We can burn messages into his back while he's here. I think the demons you play poker with tonight would like a gift. Better than wine." Wretch grabbed a *crème brûlée* torch.

"Let's wait until tonight to do the carving. I don't want the bar smelling like burnt demon before dinner."

This time, I did hear Greg laugh. He shifted back to human and inspected the frozen demon.

"His eyes follow me. It's creepy," he said.

Grace and George returned, checking him out, as well.

"If I kick him now, can he feel it?" she asked.

"Yes. He can't do anything about it," Wretch answered.

"Then, it's no fun." She satisfied herself by smacking him across the face before going behind the bar.

The afternoon proved uneventful. Even with word of a frozen demon in the club, we did our normal business rush that afternoon. The club closed between four p.m. and seven p.m. each day to clear out the demons, clean the air, and give us time to prepare for the night crowd.

I went home to clean up and found myself sitting on my bed. I could smell her. A hundred years was a long time to miss someone's scent. It hadn't changed. I still sat there when Greg came looking for me.

"She really did a number on you," he said.

"Twice." He was easy to talk to.

"My high school girlfriend hurt me so bad, I still haven't recovered. I didn't even shift on her."

He alluded to Wretch's mid-orgasmic shift with Angie.

A faraway look clung to him. "She went out with me for three years because her parents paid her. When we were ostracized from the local Canadian pack, her father, who tried to keep us in, felt guilty. I found out when we graduated she'd been seeing someone else the entire time and was engaged, with the wedding planned for the next week."

"Damn."

"Fifteen years ago, and I still want to strangle someone." He leaned against the door jam.

He was wider than me in human form. Grace assured me he was gorgeous. I didn't know of any women in his life. His duties included running with the pack each month. Dale wasn't letting him get all that far away. I hoped he got laid, then. Otherwise, he'd explode. Dr. Brun gave his wolf DNA boosts all through his developmental years. It would take a strong woman to keep up with him now.

"Tanith left me a hundred years ago. You see the residual effects."

We fell silent, each contemplating the ways women grabbed our hearts and never let go. I rarely got involved with anyone who threatened my independence. Some demon women I'd dated during my rebellious stage had had a chance at my heart. I'd pulled back each time, Wretch's family being a lesson in demon-dragon birth control—the same message Obsidian wanted sent, and the entire paranormal community never forgot.

"No wonder Grace feels safe around us," he said, smirking.

"Wretch hit on her once. She hit him back. He never did it again, as far as I know. She dates from time to time, brings them by the club for our approval."

"Do you ever approve?"

"No." *Fuck, no.*

He chuckled. "I didn't think so."

"It doesn't stop her." We'd had to pull her of a club before when the guys got carried away.

"I'm going to Vegas with you, aren't I?"

"Yes."

He nodded. "I'm your bodyguard; I can't leave you."

"I don't need a bodyguard."

"I tried to explain that to Dale. He wouldn't hear it. Seems he'd rather I risk my life with you than put the pack in danger. I still feel it's necessary to remind you that's why I'm here."

"I talked to him, Greg. He believes you're safer with us."

"That's twisted." He looked relieved.

"Yeah, but true."

He shook his head and left the room.

I refused to be grounded for two centuries. The more Wretch and I stayed outside of New Orleans while maintaining control, demons would play their games elsewhere.

I changed into actual clothing. Magical clothing could be nice, but didn't have the texture I wanted. It all felt soft and supple; sometimes, I wanted the pull of tight jeans across my abdomen and the rough feel of a starched collar on my neck.

Deep blue, buttoned-down shirt on, I opened the top three buttons. It was hot, the air outside steamy. My jeans clung to me but I didn't care. After Tanith's visit, I wanted women to appreciate my ass.

A century of trying to screw her out of my thoughts ruined in one day.

Chapter Eight

The poker game started around eleven that night with the stakes rising at each turn. A small group of older demons sat around in the back of a friend's bar on Bourbon Street. Liquor flowed freely; I checked repeatedly to make sure I could shift. Bravado filled the room as I tanked the first few hands.

Overconfident demons became chatty demons. I waited until two of the four spelled the liquor to mimic intoxication. The idea of intentionally losing brainpower at any time, much less when playing poker, made no sense to me. Why would you cripple yourself?

"Be careful those aren't the laced drinks I've heard about," I teased as two of them spelled themselves tipsy.

Three centuries-old demons ignored me, but the fourth's focus landed on me and stayed.

"What do you know about laced drinks?"

Shuffling the cards, I kept my eyes down and listened for changes in his breathing pattern. "Only that weak demons use spelled drinks to control humans. There's a batch out west making its way through the Vegas party scene."

"You don't know anything." His breath came out slow and deliberate.

I'd hit a nerve. "I want to make sure the amateurs in Vegas know that if one drop of that stuff hits New Orleans, I'll rip my way through the local population. There's no mercy for drugging humans, ever. Even if your target is shifters." They knew the laws.

"Who says we're drugging humans?" The spelled demon on my right must be feeling the effects of his drink. His words weren't slurred as much as garbled.

"Shush, we know the laws." Whispered words from across the table cut off his ability to talk. They came from a demon who kept his sobriety and anger behind a furious expression.

I looked over to see he'd sewn the talkers' lips shut. Nice move.

"Well, of course you're not. Drugging shifters is something experienced dealers wouldn't do. Only beginners would give another race the ability to see demons as they materialize." I tried to sound cavalier.

"Are you calling us amateurs?" The intense demon grasped his cards, bending the corners.

"No, older demons would use drugs to go after enemies. Drugs are the weapons for the weak, intellectually challenged magic user." That ought to get his attention.

It did.

"I'm not weak." He lowered his voice.

"But you are stupid," one of the others teased him. "You just admitted your part. Death will come by dragon, for you."

The guilty demon shoved his chair back from the table, standing up. I expected him to shift and attack me. Instead, he vanished. Hard to nail down guilty demons. A camera in the ceiling of this room would help with disputes. The owner never looked at the recording unless asked.

I'd found out what I needed to know—the aim was to drug shifters, not humans. I could understand how demons assumed the large men in gyms must be shifters; not the human anatomy we'd come to expect over centuries. The ability to bulk up the human form to sizes that made werewolves look weak came as a new development in their species.

"I guess the game is over."

Another demon stumbled back, knocking his chair over.

His friends laughed as they again spelled their liquor. I never forgot how deadly demons were, even when they acted like human college kids on spring break. This crew could have some of the drug on them. I didn't want to find out unwillingly what my reaction would be.

"What is the name of the demon dealer?" I grabbed one of the others by the collar.

"You'll never find Drake." He rolled his eyes, laughing. "He's different."

He'll die the same as the rest. No demon is that different. All of their heads are removable.

The demons left in the room with me tried to vanish but couldn't. I'd never seen that in an uninjured demon. Wretch and I had both beaten them until they were too impaired to vanish. It had to be the drug. Did they need to drink it for the effect? Or was working with it enough to change inherent magic?

"Let's try again," one said, trying to vanish. His arm disappeared and reappeared within seconds.

"My turn." Another one's leg dematerialized, returning moments later.

They stumbled into each other, laughing. I opened the door to the back alley, shoving them outside. They could play out there all night.

Closing the door, I turned to find Aaron behind me. He owned the place—one of the local werewolves who enjoyed the nightlife. Adam set him up with the bar a few years ago. My club being strictly for paranormals, any information from humans was gathered here at Aaron's place.

I hadn't needed to come to him for intel until Adam died. The deceased alpha made sure Wretch heard all of the pertinent reports coming out of here. It looked like I'd be attending more card games in this back room. I'd warn Wretch and get him to hijack Aaron's security camera to make sure we kept copies of everything.

Aaron ran a hand through his greying black hair. He had to look up to see me, his bulk indicating his dedication to the gym life.

I hadn't seen him in a few months. "I'm sorry about your alpha."

A flicker of grief flashed in his green eyes. "He was a good man and a great wolf. If this demon who ripped him and Mike apart can be stopped, I believe, as does most of the pack, that you and Wretch are the best equipped."

It didn't matter how many times the pack told me that. I'd still would've appreciated someone else taking Obsidian and Nitha down. "I appreciate it." I didn't know what else to say.

"I watched the feed just in case it got ugly. They're selling drugs?" He looked concerned, glancing over his shoulder to the room full of humans and shifters drinking behind him.

"It sounded like they are intentionally drugging shifters. I'll look into it when I'm in Vegas."

If they could get shifters addicted to drugs, letting them think they could wipe out demons…then what? Adding DNA-laced drugs? It would require Kragen and Obsidian together to pull that off. As much as I doubted it, greed and power might make them cooperate. Until one took the other out.

"Anything that affects us will do the same to them. Only worse." Aaron worried.

Human metabolisms took longer to process everything, even water. "Which might explain why we have a missing human in Vegas. Apparently, he's large enough to appear shifter to an inexperienced demon."

"Any human involved with one of us would be an easy target. Especially following sex. The scents would be strong and hard to distinguish." He licked his lips.

It looked like the wolf had a date set up for the evening. "This Drake. You heard of him before? Seen him around?"

"Yeah, he's local. Not a bad type, for a demon. Likes to play cards but doesn't cheat. He has a hand in almost every regular game I know of. If he's involved, I seriously doubt it's in distribution. My guess, he's the information guy. Making sure no one gets nosy and starts asking questions." He smiled larger as he spoke.

Drake's name sounded familiar. I didn't want Aaron to know I'd heard it before. I had to start keeping information close.

"Like I just did." I laughed. "I'm heading out with Wretch and Greg. My absence may quell any concerns tonight raised. Hopefully. We'll be back in a few days."

"I have a weekly game in three nights. He's always here for it. I sit in from time to time. I'll let you know if he says anything."

He was a good friend. I appreciated those every day now. "Thanks, Aaron. I'll contact you when I get back."

Walking back to my club, I enjoyed the sounds of parties. The last time I'd had a carefree time with friends felt like years ago. Letting my guard down to have fun wasn't an option. Not with Obsidian out there, with Nitha a minor annoyance compared to her mother. The impulsive, psychotic daughter left trails leading back to her, daring us to run to the demon council with something and report it. Up until recently, she hadn't been punished because her mother sat on the Arcane Court and pulled favors, or threatened other members, to keep the sentencing minor.

The removal of her magic had made her more dangerous, though. I knew this now. Until then, she'd been the spoiled child of an ancient demon. Removal of powers amounted to the worst punishment for a demon, including death. They called it shadowing. The demon became a shadow, something that could be ignored; without magic, they were still immortal and extremely strong. But in the paranormal world, they were vulnerable.

Turning shifters into demons worked better than human transformations. Shifters already had the ability to change shape. The addition of different forms would be a tweak to the DNA. I'd have to ask Angie, but I bet the changes in Greg's DNA allowed him to change into other forms, but as a born werewolf, he always shifted into a wolf out of habit. He would freak out if I told him he might be part demon. It would put a price on his head; as high, if not higher, than Wretch's. My possible change to demon had been bandied about for centuries; the reality wouldn't shock those who wanted me dead for other reasons.

A demon werewolf would be as dangerous as Wretch. The three of us, at full power, would be unstoppable, even by Obsidian. A fight I longed to have but it would be years before we were ready. George, with his demon DNA changes, could be our fourth. Given the recent blow to my organization, it looked like we were stronger than ever. It honored the sacrifices of Adam and Mike.

"Hello, sexy. You look miles away."

A woman appeared in front of me, a sexy, dirty blonde with curves popping out of her corset.

Tempted, I still needed to move on. "No, thank you, beautiful. A rain check?" I wanted her number.

"Are you sure you don't want to chat? My body's not being offered right now. My shoulder is." She tilted her head, smiling.

The seduction I'd assumed was clearly in my mind. Her posture and scent filling every intake of breath spoke of compassion, not intimacy. "I'm sorry." Damn, I was clumsy with women.

"Well, I did dress my breasts up, posing them for licking. It's not my normal state of dress. I'm Elise." She held out her hand.

I took her hand in mine. Small and warm, with a firm grip. "I'm Cimmerian. You can call me Cim."

"Like simulation?" She bit her lip, fighting a grin.

Laughing, I realized she must be a technology savvy woman. Wretch talked this way often. I would try to keep up. "Yes, with a C."

"What do you do, Cim with a C?"

Somehow, she'd managed to move next to me and grasp my elbow with her hand. My intuition told me to be on guard. She was making assumptions normally left to lovers.

We walked toward my club. "I own a club by the Market." My arm tugged as she stopped in her tracks.

"The one rumored to house werewolves and demons?"

Her look seemed genuine and serious. Practiced spy moves. I didn't trust her.

"I've heard those rumors myself." I could walk around the truth for years.

"Then you should know, Cim with C, that our meeting tonight was not accidental. I'm a professor at Uppsala University…"

That's the accent I noticed barely behind her perfect English. She was Swedish.

"...studying forensic archeology." She peeked up at me intently. "For the past five hundred years."

My surprise stayed momentary. My awkwardness around women didn't interfere with my ability to read people; only my ability to seduce them wantonly. "You hide your scent well."

A smile stretched across her face. "Thank you. I've been working on pheromones in my spare time."

"So you're a chemist, as well?" I wondered why I didn't pull away. My life didn't allow for assumptions anymore, even the small ones that make flirtations so enticing. "Who sent you?"

She checked her watch. "Under five minutes, your mother told me you'd ask."

My mother. She'd never sent a woman my way. Who wouldn't know that? Kragen? This Drake?

"A Swedish dragon. My mother has changed her taste in future daughters-in-law."

She covered her mouth in a lousy attempt at coy. "I've been in Scandinavia for six hundred years, Cimmerian, Death Dealer, eternal bachelor. I'm a dragon, the great-granddaughter of the eldest Scandinavian dragon who resides in the mountains protecting our legacy."

If true, someone had infiltrated the Norse dragons. A huge problem. I'd have to speak to Kellen in Vegas about it—his family was from Stockholm.

She took a moment to gather her thoughts. "With Nitha over in Europe, we have a chance to remove her mother's influence from the states. The Court believes you're the best dragon for that job. I work for them, to answer your next question. This is a favor to your mother, as well, but the Court asked me to stop by. Apparently, two dragons in town are better than one."

The Court appointed only one dragon per large city on purpose. It had to be Drake; Kragen would've prepped her better.

Elise barely came up to my chest. Small for a dragon—dainty, some might say—but I felt the strength in her grip on my arm. I slowed my pace to extend our time together.

She slipped her hand around my bicep. We turned toward Jackson Square, the church spires in the distance lit by moonlight.

Elise kept reciting the script she'd been given about the Court. She didn't know we'd found out who the new member was.

"You don't know?" She laughed.

"No."

"Kragen." Her expression fluctuated between pity and amusement.

I played along. "A drug dealer."

"The oldest known dealer," she whispered.

"Someone you knew?"

"A human friend. Centuries ago, before human medicine could help her survive withdrawal." Mourning laced her voice.

"I'm sorry." I glanced down at her, taking in the beauty with immense brains by my side. Her blonde hair began dark at the roots, growing more golden as it traveled down her back. Her curves barely fit in her corset. Her jeans clung to a soft, rounded belly and ass. Today's human media would call her fat; I knew she was stunning. No way it could be a coincidence she showed up the same day Tanith did.

"You like curves, Death Dealer." She was playing with me.

"Very much." My body screamed its approval, unseen in my jeans, but I'm sure my quicker breathing gave it away.

"Thank you." She blushed, licking her lips.

My desire tried to leap as I held it in check.

She must've felt my arm flinch. "Not tonight, sexy dragon. I've only arrived and I'm not a conquest for a night."

Nodding, I agreed completely. "What is your position with the Court?"

"I'm new to the job, appointed twenty years ago. Your mother is worried you've taken on too many non-dragons. She mentioned a few shifters, not by name." Again, she bit her lip.

It made me very suspicious. A centuries-old dragon female doesn't play coy without an agenda. I didn't know what she'd been told, but her actions had me more wary that turned on. "I have a team here. My mother knows less of them than she wants. The three shifters who work with me are tough, seasoned, and I'd trust them with my life." I tried to keep the anger from my voice.

She noticed it, anyway. "I didn't mean to insult you. It's possible your mother was trying to justify sending another person your way when you already have a strong team."

I doubted it. "It's possible."

We walked across the square in silence. Wretch would have her history and full biography in minutes when I introduced them. The next few days, we could keep an eye on her through local contacts without this luscious body distracting my judgment.

I knew when my desire wanted to overrule my sense. This woman's kiss, I was sure, would turn my brain off. A luxury item I couldn't afford. If anything else, Tanith's reappearance today reminded me of the price I'd pay.

The street in front of the club was full of demons shouting.

"This can't be good."

"I'll never get used to excited demon stench." Her eyes darted like she expected to see someone she knew.

"Let's see what's going on." I looked up to find Wretch on the second floor balcony outside my office. He made an hourglass gesture with his hands. There didn't appear to be any concern from him.

We skirted the group, hugging the windows, coming out on the other side to see two demons shifting rapidly. A contest. Someone from the crowd called out an animal and they would see who could shift faster. A nice game, but one that shouldn't happen in public. I guessed that was why Wretch stood upstairs. Keeping an eye out for curious humans.

Once inside, George eyed Elise as Grace pretended not to.

"George, Grace, this is Elise. She's been sent by the Court to train with us." They knew that meant to be wary.

"Nice to meet you." She reached out, placing her hand in George's extended one. It barely covered his palm. "You're a big one, aren't you?"

He flushed. We really needed to get him more experience with women.

Grace noticed it, as well. "Hello, Elise. I'm Grace. I'm a jaguar shifter and run this place. This is George. He's a gentle giant gorilla shifter. Women confuse him. Often." Her smile lit up her whole face. It was fake, her sense of people as exact as mine.

George withdrew his hand politely. "Boss, should we stop the game?" He nodded outside.

"Yes. Even with Wretch upstairs watching, there are too many cell phones with video. We couldn't explain this." I stepped aside as he made his way out.

"He's huge." Elise watched him go. "Remind me not to make him angry."

"He body-slammed Obsidian into a concrete wall." Grace's response meant to warn as well as inform.

Elise paused for a moment, thinking. "You know, trapping her in concrete for eternity doesn't sound like a bad idea."

"I'm sure Cim needs to have a chat upstairs with Uncle Fester. Why don't we have coffee and a chat?" Grace wanted to grill her.

Elise hesitated, looking at me.

"Go ahead." I stared at the jaguar.

Grace stuck her tongue out at me. "Treat me like a teenager. Go ahead."

I laughed. "I need to talk to Wretch. You two don't embarrass George."

Walking upstairs, I passed a shadow that was there and then gone. I'd have Wretch check the video feed when we got back.

I found him seated on the window settee. "Who's the lovely woman with the almost undetectable accent?"

"Elise. Dragon, Court member for twenty years. She claims my mother sent her. I don't trust her." I lowered my voice, glaring at him. "Speak."

"The sexy dragon downstairs, now that's a story." He licked his lips. "Obviously a plant. Whoever hurt Tanith had to notice her safe return. Do we keep her close, and if so, how close?"

"No fucking informants."

He stood up, walking over to me, laughing. "Did you sense magic when she approached you? Did she shift to prove to you she's dragon?"

"Given my reaction, I'm concerned. Obviously, my objectivity is compromised. I want a full report on Elise as soon as you can get one. Birth parents, education, known associates, credit card receipts, bank accounts, everything."

Wretch wrote down the list I wanted. "You'll have it before we leave. Does she know?"

"No. The trip, our reasons for it, everything. Grace will watch her while we're gone."

"You should know we might lose Grace this year." He sat back down, lounging in his open-to-the-waist, buttoned-down shirt and linen pants. He looked like a porn star during a break in filming.

I bristled at the thought. "Predicting death is not one of your better talents."

"Her new boyfriend." He waited for it to sink in. "Her mother set them up."

Damn interfering mothers. I'd sent Grace out of town when Obsidian was here to protect her. Seems it worked. If she left to mate, it would keep her safe. "I won't stand in her way. Proximity to us—"

"—is deadly." He nodded. "It's all set for Vegas. I called the pilot; the jet will be ready when we are. We need to find Billy. If he can get her out of our danger zone, it'd be best."

At that thought, I felt an urge to shift. Rolling my shoulders back, I realized they were tight and tense. I needed it. The thought barely passed through my mind when my vision changed. "That's new."

"Your new powers allow you to shift with a thought. It's what we've seen in both George and Greg. The longer demon powers run through you, the faster your shifts will be." He walked around behind me. "You're still deep purple. You have new spikes on your back between your wings. Spread them out to the walls."

They felt heavier as I reached out to either side. "They're on your joints, as well."

I bent in my right wing to look at the highest tip. Pushing the joint down to eye height, I saw the spikes. Small, black, and sharp. Demon spikes. It would be impossible to hide my emerging hybrid status if anyone looked close enough. "I wonder if I can pull those in." I focused on them and they disappeared.

"Good. It'll help us keep that to ourselves for a while." Wretch walked back to my front, shifting to an identical dragon form. "If you shift with spikes and I'm nearby, I'll shift without them. We fight enough alike to keep enemies confused. If Obsidian finds out you're already gaining demon characteristics, she'll ignore the agreement and come after you."

"Why? You're safe around her, most of the time."

"She believes I'm weak and need you to back me up. You scare her, Cim. Dragon strength is the one thing we can't have. Our inherent power comes from magic, not anatomy. We are no more physically gifted than the average werewolf. It's the demon ability to shift using magic that has kept us alive. If dragons gain the power to use demon magic, they will be the strongest species on the planet. That would change the dynamics completely. Removing our assumed place at the top of the food chain. In fact, I'm positive your absorption of demon magic triggered this particular obsession. In her mind, she believes the only way to compete is to demonize other shifters."

Shifting back to human, I thought of the consequences. I'd been told my whole life demons were the predators and every other living thing prey. Period. It didn't matter which species—all of them bowed to demons. Obsidian's obsessive need to turn shifters wouldn't be necessary if she didn't feel threatened. Her love of torture could continue unabated for generations in Asia. The ability to appear and disappear at will allowed her to kidnap millions from poorer countries like North Korea or rural China without ever being detected. "Extinction of the human race."

"Exactly. Your transformation, which I'm sure she's going to figure out, if she hasn't already, proves it's possible." He walked to his office.

I spelled my same clothing from earlier while following him. "Elise said her great-grandmother is the eldest Scandinavian dragon."

"A perfect fit. Genetically, that is. Sounds way too planned." He grinned. Finding threats before they knew we'd figured them out made him happy.

Downstairs, we heard the ladies laughing. A nice change from the usual arguments. Even George and Grace, left alone long enough, would fill the place with pheromones.

"Damn, Grace. Again?" George's voice carried as he came upstairs. In Wretch's office, he found a large chair. "Cim, your lady friend is charming. Grace is telling her stories I thought were private." He thought of her as a sister.

I couldn't tell if he approved. "Elise...what do you think?"

"She's perfect for you. I'm guessing in your world that's not a good thing." The gorilla shifter laughed.

"Too perfect is usually a set-up. We have to find Grace's boyfriend while we're gone. George, keep an eye on her. I'm afraid he's either dead or has betrayed her by now."

Wretch looked at my concerned expression. "She's going to be fine, *dad*. We can send her back to Mexico, hopefully, before this drug business wanders into town."

"I hope so. She hates when I send her away." Which I'd only had to do twice. Each time, she'd returned within days.

George coughed. "Boss, she wanted to leave after Laythe was killed. It's why she took off without an argument. Being there while Obsidian dismembered Adam and Mike was the last for her. She didn't tell you. Although, if Billy's dead, she might be pissed enough to stay and fight."

No one, especially me, would blame her for that. The bloody scene still woke me at night. Some days, I could smell blood as I walked through the front door. Greg and George did, too. We chose not to talk about it.

They had personal stakes in this as their DNA had been altered during childhood. Grace, and Angie, were the true innocents in our group. Their safety should come first.

"Do I need to tell her to go?" I wondered aloud.

Wretch laughed. "You know better. She'll make the right choice."

I glanced at George, wondering if he could run the club on his own.

He seemed to follow my thoughts. "I'll learn everything she does, every moment while you two kick ass in Vegas. After all, when you come back, you'll be spending more time here every day and can correct me if I screw up."

Upon hearing the door close downstairs, I excused myself from my two amused friends and left.

Elise sat in one of the two booths up front, watching the street. "It's nice here."

"The river is a short walk out front, the shops over there." I pointed to the closed-up Market. "Teeming with people every day. I like it."

"Grace cleaned up and left. She's very funny and welcoming." Her hands twisted a napkin. Another nervous tell.

"Why are you really here?" I sat across from her.

"I'm just nervous about being alone with you. I've never been out of Europe. Sure, we've visited the states a few times, but I always had my brothers or my parents with me. This is a little intimidating." She chewed her bottom lip.

She wasn't any good at deception. Even she didn't believe the words coming out of her mouth. "Where are you staying?"

"On Royal Street. It's a condo a couple of blocks from here. Guessing from our walk."

"Sorry, didn't realize you were so new to the area. Would you like me to walk you home?" She'd walked next to me like someone familiar with the streets. She had to be with Drake.

Her eyes lit up when she smiled. Blue eyes got me every time. Wishing I could enjoy her body before we exposed her, I called up to Wretch locking the door behind me. We walked in silence, her hand in the crook of my arm. The two blocks went quickly.

She made the decision for me. "Yes, your mother thinks we'd be good together. It doesn't mean we have to give in to anything. In fact, I'd like to get a chance to know everyone here first. I don't want your friends treating me different because I'm your girl. I want them to respect me as I learn to help out."

I'm your girl?

This was not a dragon. No female dragon refers to herself that way. We needed to keep her close. She smelled like a dragon but if Obsidian had been experimenting on her, there was no way for me to tell what she was until she shifted. "Then goodnight, Elise. I'll contact you in a few days."

"I left my number with Grace. George has it, too." She stood up on her toes, kissing my cheek.

She smelled good. My body and brain were going to fight. I liked those fights; made me feel alive.

I watched her hips sway up to the front door. On the way back to the club, I noticed a couple of demons studying me.

"Anything I can help you boys with?" I started shifting the moment I reached some shadows.

I recognized one of the demons from earlier tonight.

"No, no, no. You don't need to drink our souls. We wanted to tell you...Harry, the guy from the poker game tonight? He only thinks he's part of the drug dealing. Someone in Vegas gives him enough information to satisfy his curiosity."

He wasn't young, at least five-hundred-years old.

"Why are you telling me this?" Tattling to me was not a demon's best move.

He shifted from foot to foot. "The new local demon lord, the guy who took over for Laythe, wants you in the loop. He thinks the group doing this is reckless and if they expose shifters to humans, which this drug might do, it would lead to them finding us."

The same thought occurred to me. "And who is this new Lord?" Pretending I didn't know things helped me learn a lot from demons.

"Luke. He transferred from Africa. He's as dangerous as Nitha, we're told, and smart. He wants to continue Laythe's relationship with you. He said it brings stability to the region." The entire time he talked, his eyes had been focused somewhere else. Luke made him memorize that speech.

"Tell him I'd like to meet him when he's in town." No doubt the Court had a say in which demon took over the area. Someone sympathetic to Nitha and Obsidian would make the entire western hemisphere unstable. Also possible he'd been put in place to keep things calm while Obsidian perfected her DNA tests. Either way, it meant things in New Orleans would settle down for the near future.

The demon shook his head. "He won't be coming here. He believes if he is seen with you, it will put a price on his life. We will find you to bring messages."

I took out a business card for the club that had Wretch's public email address on it. "Give him this. The mailbox is secure and monitored daily. He can reach us faster than sending you two to find me. If you need to get me in person, you know where I live." We'd never return his call.

"Laythe's house," they said in unison.

"Yes. Leave a message in the mailbox or on the porch." These two were old enough to stay hidden, even in daylight.

They vanished. I hated that. The coolest demon power was vanishing—I'd wanted it. Until I was told I may have the ability. Then, I started worrying about reappearing somewhere in pieces, or not at all.

It didn't help my suspicions of Elise that these demons stood outside of her place. In fact, it made me certain she worked for Drake. Not a subtle move. I'd grown used to the deception of Wretch's family, who, as evil as they were, knew how to infiltrate a group of friends.

Elise? Too obvious.

Chapter Nine

I settled into the couch on the luxury jet. Wretch called ahead. My protests went ignored as he wanted to see if Greg would be tempted back to using. The werewolf understood my concerns, trying not to smile at the realization he would be free in Vegas.

Calling Tanith to warn her occurred to me and then quickly got dismissed. Wretch's casual lean across from me raised my suspicions. "What did you do?"

"I called her, lover boy." He patted me on the shoulder.

My bags fit under the pull-out table. "Why?"

"You wouldn't." He sounded confident.

It irritated me. "Of course I would."

"You don't have her number." He held up his phone, forgetting I'd called her earlier. Him distracted wasn't good.

"She gave it to me before she left. Actually, she programmed it into my phone under 'Hottest Bitch I'll Ever Get'." Annoyingly correct.

"It doesn't mean anything." He gnawed his lip.

Worry wasn't normal for him. "I got the message a century ago." The fact I hadn't fallen in love since then must be beside the point.

"You need to get laid during this trip."

Wretch's solution for everything, including world peace.

"I plan on it." Lying was not normal for me.

"So do I." Greg perked up, reminding me of an eager puppy.

"Elise." Even though I knew she was a plant, I wanted to be proven wrong.

Wretch laughed. "Drake is sloppy. I checked to make sure it was unintentional. Pictures of him and Elise together are the first things that pop up when you search for them. She's one of his women. There are no pictures of her shifting, ever. I'm sure she's part human; hence, the lack of demon smell."

Greg sat up. "Human or shifter? I didn't think human women could survive the pregnancy?"

"They survive the pregnancy. They can't shift when the child rips their way out of the womb." I'd seen a demon birth once. It proved enough.

The wolf paused. "That's brutal."

"We are," Wretch answered. "Elise wouldn't smell like a demon but has all of the characteristics of one. The less shifting she does, the longer her humanness is maintained. It's the same with your use of demon strength when you shift. If you shift less often, the demon DNA sits dormant. That's why Angie had to test you and George at the genetic level."

"I need a date," I said too loudly. Today had taught me I'd like to have a woman in my life.

"I can arrange that," Wretch said.

"No, the last woman you set me up with was a set of rare demon twins. I almost died." The shifting possibilities had been quite delectable, though.

Greg perked up. "Demons come in twins?"

Wretch would've told him how rare it was but he couldn't stop laughing.

The pilot made her announcement and the sole flight attendant demonstrated the safety equipment.

Apparently, she knew Wretch. "Use the seat belts, though I know you won't. In case of water landing, shift and fly your horny ass to safety. Carry the mutt with you."

She smelled of angry cat. My friend left broken hearts inside angry females across the globe.

He met her glare with a smirk.

"No drinking, smoking, or shifting into creatures grabbing me from behind."

A threat he would ignore, judging from the smile on his face.

"You make an impression." I had to laugh.

He was proud. "Fuck yeah, with eight arms."

Her stare cut through Wretch's jovial attitude.

Greg coughed, averting his eyes from hers. "Is there anyone you haven't...?"

Wretch turned to him. "I haven't been in Asia for five hundred years, Australia in one hundred fifty or so. My shifter conquests there are either dead or too old for you."

"I'm amazed you don't have hundreds of children." The werewolf sounded impressed, and unaware of the difference between sexual compatibility and procreative viability.

"Thousands." The demon hybrid corrected. "Because I always use protection. You've met my family."

"Yes." Greg looked down. "If we kill Nitha and Obsidian, you can have a family."

"That's been mentioned before." His mood sat there on his face, heard in the growl.

We fell silent.

I took the time to look around. He'd updated the plane since I'd been in it last. I preferred to travel at night by air. Riding the wind exhilarated me. It was a luxurious private jet with leather seats, couches, marble counter tops, and gold fixtures in the kitchen. Internet access allowed us to pull up local Vegas news. He decided we should fly in luxury instead of just appearing in his penthouse suites. After all, why have gorgeous material things if they sit gathering dust in an airport hangar?

"Would they report local drug use at gyms?" Greg burped his appreciation for the drinks before diving into the food the stewardess dropped in front of him.

"Not likely. They might say something about missing people. The paranormal community in Begs is large. Most mingle freely with humans undetected. If shifters go missing, their human friends might report them. Other shifters, or demons, even, would contact Kellen."

I'd texted him during the limo ride to the airport, including about Elise claiming the same family tree.

"I left him a message. Haven't heard back yet." Wretch stretched out on the couch, focusing most of his attention on the flight attendant. That must've been one hell of a flight.

"He won't answer you." Kellen hated Wretch. "I sent a message, too."

All members of the Court and their employees had a special contact list on their phones. Mine came preloaded as my skills with phones, or any electronics, lay in destruction, not use. I sent another text message.

The second largest dragon shifter in the US called right back. "Tell that juvenile friend of yours that I don't give status reports to sidekicks."

"Hello, Kellen." I winked at Greg.

He ignored me. "Do you know he left a fax message at my house? Anyone could've picked that up."

Not good. "You faxed him?"

"He won't give me his phone number. Unless he wants me to keep sending messages coded as love letters from his wife…" Wretch licked his lips, causing goose bumps on the attendant's arms. Her name tag read 'Irene Rubin.'

Kellen heard the exchange, sputtering in reply. "One of my girlfriends left me because of his game. Tell the freak I want to talk to you only. Now. Cim, it's bad here. All of my demon contacts are missing. Nightly poker games at the casino are human and shifter only. Something is way off."

"There's a new drug in town. Distributed in drinks for gym rats. Tanith knows about it. She showed up at my place covered in welts with the drug in the wounds. Her human boyfriend is missing." Tanith liked Kellen; she thought of him as family.

"How long before you get here?" He would plan our next moves.

"A few hours. We'll get settled in the Sky Suites first. We may be in town for a while."

"Tanith could've told me something was going on. Not come to you."

He should be angry; he wasn't. His patience got him the job in Vegas.

"Go easy on her; she's scared. I've never seen her this way before." Which bothered me immensely. I wanted to rush to her aid and yet, I could still recall her screaming form hovering over me.

"Contact me when you get here. We can walk City Center. You'll feel the difference." He'd made that place his home base. With a casino, hotels, and residences all within walking distance, he heard more than he would on the streets.

Wretch listened to the conversation. "Is there anything else I should do now?"

I wanted to smack the smirk off his face. "No."

Grace called from the club to say all was okay, New Orleans quiet. Either we didn't notice something going on—unlikely —or Kellen's disappearing demons could be connected. I told her to look out for dwindling demon stench.

With two hours left in the flight, Wretch excused himself to the back with his phone. I assumed he called Angie.

Greg helped the flight attendant clean up the mess we'd left from food. She seemed to warm up to him.

He sat back down next to me. "Tanith."

"Yes." The hairs on my arms stood up.

"How long did you two date?" If he was interested in her, and most males were, he hid it well behind a concerned expression.

"Fifty years on and off." A hundred years ago.

He tried to hide his surprise. "That's a long time."

"Neither of us was easy to catch." I loved it.

"Then she left you?" The expression on his face mirrored mine at the time.

"At the altar." In Wretch's backyard, with my parents standing there.

"Ouch."

"I healed."

He looked confused. "She ever explain?"

"No." I'd been afraid to ask.

Wretch came back in. "She pulled a dozen scales from his chest, trying to yank his heart out." He paused for effect. "Took me an hour to push everything back in."

"Holy shit!" Greg squirmed in his seat.

"Maybe I'll ask her why she stopped. Wretch, here, didn't arrive for a while." A time period where I'd decided my heart would remain in my chest, in every way.

"She won't talk." My friend hated her for hurting me. He made himself a drink, ignoring the glare he got from the flight attendant, and shifted to completely naked human.

Her expression softened. I couldn't see the front side but I'm sure he'd magically helped himself to a few inches. They walked to the back bedroom together.

"He's a slut." Greg sounded surprised.

"For all time."

As we fell silent, I remembered my non-wedding night. Wretch had planned the ceremony, his backyard draped in flowers, security cameras running with full color and sound. My parents flew in the night before, soaring over the Mississippi River right up to the French Quarter.

Tanith had met them dozens of times over the previous century and they adored her, as I did. The preparations for her dress had been kept secret from me but Laythe assured me it was stunning. Two days prior, Tanith began acting different. I'd brushed it off as nerves. I shouldn't have.

The party started at three in the afternoon, with her limo driving up to the curb thirty minutes later. She wasn't in it. Scared she'd been hurt, we began searching for her. None of our local contacts knew anything and the marriage had been common knowledge. The first decade of the twentieth century, our planning intentional.

She'd vanished the night before. No one had seen her since the bridal dinner her friends threw. I lived part-time in the warehouse then and fell asleep with the doors open, hoping she'd come home. I longed to wake with her next to me.

The sound of unintelligible screaming tore me out of slumber. The pain in my chest didn't register immediately. I attempted to get up. Tanith sat on my torso in dragon form, pulling scales from my body. I found out later I'd shifted to dragon form when she clawed a hole in my human chest.

I had frozen in place. No amount of effort moved my arms or legs…my voice trapped inside of me as my mouth failed to open. I'd been spelled immobile. She spoke in a language I'd heard in Europe centuries before, older than humanity. With eyes glazed over, she'd stared at my face with a complete lack of recognition.

A noise from the roof spooked her; she stopped, tilting her head to listen, and then ran out of the door, slamming it behind her.

The sounds from the back bedroom on the plane brought me back. I'd tried to adopt Wretch's cavalier attitude toward sex in the years following. It turned out not to be me.

The pilot announced our descent as the two emerged from the bedroom. As soon as the woman returned to her duties, Wretch dialed the limo service for pickup. I'd packed an overnight bag, the condos stocked with everything we'd need. Including clothes. Greg's bag was larger, the trip scheduled too fast to stock up the room where he'd be staying.

***

The smell of fresh-baked croissants greeted me as I entered the penthouse. Placing my bag on one bed, I admired the view. I could see for miles from up here, the closest I could get to flying in Vegas. Here, someone would shoot me down.

Kellen picked his phone up on the first ring. "Tanith said you're to leave her out of it. But please find her boyfriend."

"Nice."

"She's scared, Cim. The hotel security is looking out for strange demon activities. We have some."

"You have that pull at a casino?" Impressive.

"I can get the local werewolf pack involved. They could prowl the casino floors, expanding our reach. If we're going to find her boyfriend alive, we need ears now."

"Good idea. We brought a wolf with us. Shifts into a small pony." Greg's size would intimidate some younger demons. I counted on it. I put the phone on speaker.

"You in Wretch's place?" He knew the answer already. It was his job.

114

I appreciated the courtesy. "Yes."

"I'm on my way up. If you'd get Wretch to hack the security cameras, we can watch the floor of the casino from there."

His mind worked like Wretch. No wonder they clashed.

"I'll set it up."

Wretch appeared in the hallway by the bar—he memorized the location of alcohol and food wherever we went.

I managed to rescue two croissants. "Have you hacked the security cameras here yet?"

"Years ago." He pointed to the television on the wall. "Channel zero is the poker room, one is the casino floor."

The television screen focused on the casino floor. My ex-fiancée paced, looking intimidating and beautiful. "Kellen said she's spooked."

Her bravado wasn't forced or fake, normally; she'd earned her confidence. Even Wretch didn't want to fight her one-on-one.

He vanished, appearing seconds later with a wet, naked, and angry werewolf. "You son of a bitch."

"Demon." Wretch corrected him.

"Whatever. Let me finish showering." He shook his head, spraying water everywhere. It looked like a shampoo commercial.

"Ten minutes." Wretch vanished with him, reappearing alone.

"Initiation into this group is a bitch." I laughed.

"Yes, it is. He's taking it better than I thought." He found more croissants in the fridge, popped them onto a tray for the oven.

I stood in front of the screen scanning for problems. Same thing I did in New Orleans but with better electronics. We really could use one of these in each poker room. It wouldn't work because I had no doubt Wretch had already thought of it. If he couldn't find a way to pull it off, it couldn't be done.

Tanith looked skittish. Subtle, but there. Her gaze scanned the floor more quickly than the environment required. Like she expected the group that had captured her to pop out of the walls, or shift, grab her, and vanish.

Wretch handed me a warm croissant. "She's still beautiful, my friend."

"And frightened," Kellen added, walking in the front door.

"I never gave you a key." Wretch glared at him.

Kellen ignored him. "I have access to all rooms in this place. Or didn't you see who the building owner was when you signed the lease?" He stood five-foot-eleven—short for a dragon, with close-cropped brown hair and light brown eyes currently looking amused.

"You said she's frightened."

He ignored Wretch, stepping around to address me. "She was pulled off the floor a week ago. We have the security footage. I'll have my team send it to you." He nodded to Wretch. "We don't recognize the demons who took her. I imagine you won't, either. It was one day before the demon pull-back in this casino. I've called the security chiefs from the other casinos and they've also seen a decrease in demon activity. If a powerful demon is running drugs, that would explain the vanishing act. Especially if they need runners and distribution centers."

"If it traces back to Kragen, it's global." Wretch pulled a wireless keyboard and mouse from under the coffee table. Turning the television screen to a computer, he pulled up the link for the file Kellen's team just sent.

The video was one minute long. We replayed it six times before Kellen stopped us. The images replayed in my memory as I tried to sort out what I'd seen. Two demons walked up to Tanith, had a short discussion, and they all vanished. She didn't appear distressed or concerned during the conversation. I didn't recognize the demons involved, which made tracking them down harder. "I don't know them. Have they shown up on your surveillance?"

Wretch filled a glass with whiskey, handing it to me. "No, I've never met them. With Obsidian holed up in Asia and Nitha in Europe, there's a slight power vacuum here. This could be a ploy by Kragen to pull in the Americas."

I doubted it. "Or this is him being a drug dealer. Nothing more."

Kellen stared hard at Wretch but no drink appeared for him. "I'm with Cim. These two are regulars in poker games. None of the security at the nearest four casinos have had trouble with them."

"New to the area?" I hoped. It would give us a trail to follow.

Kellen extinguished it. "No, they've been coming here for thirty years."

Wretch poured a glass of whiskey, stopping short of handing it to the Swedish dragon. "And?"

"They are small-time gamblers. Never bet more than the highest rolling human at the table. Some nights that's a grand; others, it's a million. Cautious, observant, and well-respected in the area. I've never had an issue with either of them fighting, using humans for more than sex partners, or shifting in the middle of games when a human obviously cheated." He smiled as the glass hit his open palm. After taking a long drink, he continued. "These two being involved makes me more concerned for her safety. It looks like she was supposed to be killed. The last few years, she's made a point to talk down her fighting skills to keep the demons from wanting to test their mettle. No way they knew she'd could take on five of them and walk away without breathing hard."

He admired her. We all did.

"She was whipped." I nodded at his startled expression. "It was laced with a drug and she didn't risk shifting. Her presence at my place was a sign of desperation. She's taking this seriously. Have you asked her anything about her capture?"

"Why don't you ask her? Weren't you two involved at one point?" He wasn't being facetious.

Most relationships between dragons begin and end amicably. We were the exception. "She left me at the altar in the evening, waking me later while ripping my heart out."

He stared at me. Disbelieving.

Wretch laughed. "She'd have succeeded if I hadn't shown up." He bowed. "There was blood everywhere."

Kellen downed his drink. "Thanks for not telling me that sooner."

"You're welcome." I covered my smile with my hand. His opinion of her would change now. Good for him. Tanith could out-wrestle this dragon and leave him bleeding out in ten minutes.

Kellen stood still.

"What?"

"If this is Kragen, how come I haven't seen Drake? His lapdog frequents casinos with samples," Kellen said.

"Some of his friends are in New Orleans right now. Including the female I mentioned, Elise. Either he's very sloppy, or he thinks I am. Her skills don't include deception or acting. Since they're a couple in public, I'd imagine he's there with her. Likely sucking up to Luke, the new local demon lord."

"Aaron believes he'll show up for a poker game in the next few days. He sits in often enough to get information without raising suspicion," I explained.

Wretch gave me a look. I guess I forgot to tell him about the braggarts at poker. He downed another drink. "If he's in New Orleans, then his operation here is headless. Kragen doesn't oversee his own warehouses. Those two who grabbed your woman should be flogged for vanishing in public. I'd report them to the Court, but Kragen now sits on it."

"Fuck, you're kidding?" Kellen hadn't heard.

"No, the demons on the Court now are Vex and Kragen."

"The oldest male demon alive, Vex, and the oldest drug dealer, Kragen. What a combination." Wretch turned the bottle up.

I was going to hate asking the question. "Out loud. The thoughts you are trying to drown, I need to hear them."

He smirked and then announced, "Didn't you know? Vex is my biological grandfather. Lover to Obsidian and father to Laythe, Nitha, and my dear, departed mother, Iona."

"No, you never told me." I got so furious I shifted.

Kellen sensed danger. "Careful, boys. This could get ugly."

I grabbed Wretch by the throat.

Wretch shifted into a huge snake and slithered out of my grasp. "At what point should I have told you both my grandparents sat on the Court? Did you think they'd assign you to me without having complete control of the demon positions?"

"Did you just spell me?" I hadn't tried to hit him in decades.

He froze in his demon dandy form. "You felt that?"

We both knew it was the new demon powers I'd absorbed. I shifted back to human, spelling clothing for myself. Greg was apparently sleeping in the shower.

Kellen looked at me, confused. "I demand an explanation."

I put a hand on his shoulder. "Demand is the wrong word."

He relaxed.

"I absorb demon magic when I suck down their souls. At times, there are side effects. It's normal. As you can tell, it even catches Wretch off-guard." Keeping my voice calm while my mind raced proved a challenge.

My best friend walked back over to the bar. "Four bottles. Two for me, one for each of you." He handed them out. "I really thought you knew, Cim. Vex and Obsidian's relationship has been common knowledge in the demon community for twenty-five-hundred years. I assumed I told you. Vex is not a problem, in that he plays for his own ends. His manipulations are strictly carnal. He wants to live long enough to enjoy every drug, woman, and drink every created."

"A demon after your own heart," I said, realizing he admired his grandfather.

"It's how he's remained happy for millennia without becoming a target. I admire that." He downed one of his bottles.

Kellen laughed. "Hell, *I* admire that." He clinked bottles with Wretch.

"I'm still not happy." I downed half of mine in one gulp.

"Of course not. You thought you had a smoking-hot Swedish dragon to play with, for a moment."

I didn't like being teased. "Demon scum."

Wretch stared at me. "Are you okay? You're acting more like me and that's not right. You didn't eat or drink anything you shouldn't have, did you?"

Running back through the day in my mind, nothing stuck out. "I ate on the plane."

"Greg!" Wretch vanished. He reappeared with a soggy, scared wolf.

"Shift to human," I ordered.

He obliged while Wretch spelled clothes for him. "I felt myself shifting in the shower. Then I heard bizarre voices in my head."

"No, he didn't!" Wretch vanished again.

Kellen and Greg stared at me. I handed my half bottle to the werewolf. His hands shook.

"Looks like that drug made it's way onto the plane," I said.

"The flight attendant," Greg growled.

I nodded, explaining to Kellen. "The woman was pissed at Wretch but happily took two hours to have sex with him. Seems she loaded the food for us with the drug."

The other dragon looked worried. "Tell me how it feels so I'll know if they get to me."

I stood still. "I can hear your breathing louder than normal. Greg is human again but the smell of wet dog is as if he never changed. It's the emotional reaction I had to Wretch that's different. I'd never lunge at him. As if my inhibitions were less."

"Like humans and alcohol?" Greg looked sideways at the now-empty bottle in his hand.

"No. Humans become less able to use their senses. I'm sharper with fewer inhibitions." That combination could get me killed fast.

"More demon." Kellen stepped back.

"It's a drug, my friend. It'll wear off." I'm not sure I believed it when I said it. He needed to hear it.

He kept moving away. "The spines on your wings when you shifted say otherwise."

"Tell him." Wretch stood behind me. "The plane was clean."

Which meant Greg's and my transformation to hybrids had picked up pace.

"Kellen, I've been taking on different characteristics since I absorbed Narran's magic. Before that, I'd get juiced for a few weeks and then it would fade away. It's been weeks, but the changes are staying longer this time." I watched Greg to see how he reacted to the news.

Kellen relaxed his shoulders. "This isn't a new thing out of the blue for you? You always change a bit with each soul you drink?"

"Yes, I always have. At first, there was no effect at all. I might have felt a little lightheaded, then it would wear off in a few hours. Over the past two hundred years, especially since I moved to New Orleans, the absorption of magic has been noticeable. I've gotten used to putting clothes on myself after shifting. That's it. I've never tried anything else. Never wanted to."

Wretch walked around me, sniffing me like I was prey. "You do smell different now. There's a strong possibility Narran was on the drug. Kragen hates my family and my uncle was hedonistic enough to do drugs, often."

That made a bit of sense to me. "What would Kragen gain by drugging your uncle?"

Wretch sat down, motioning us to join him. "I haven't figured that out yet. It could be the two of them liked hanging out. It's not like my aunt lived in the castle with her husband. Narran's place was known for extravagant parties filled with drunk or drugged human and shifter women."

"Kragen's crowd," Kellen added.

"Yes," Wretch agreed. "It could be anything from their pasts. The one demon I suspect would know is Vex. He won't talk. He's the originator of a personal agenda. His entire relationship with Obsidian was self-preservation."

"Did he think giving her kids would keep him alive?" I remember her holding me in the air as Wretch killed Dr. Brun, her late human husband. She'd enjoyed it.

"It worked. Unlike the twisted doctor, Vex is a demon. I would be surprised if he doesn't have a few dozen bits of information on her she doesn't want made public. They were together when the Mongols ran wild. Even she has secrets," Wretch explained.

I didn't doubt she had them. After seeing her fight, I sensed she wouldn't care. Killing was an art form to her. I ripped off heads, drank souls, and fought any demon that pissed me off. While I loved my job, Wretch and I anticipated the after-work entertainment. The best way to close off a day of fighting evil was enjoying curvy human women after winning money at a poker game.

Greg stayed silent during the entire conversation. I'm sure he heard every word. Keeping track of the complicated, almost inbred, relationships of demons would lengthen his life.

The place smelled like shifters and testosterone. "Air freshener." I headed to the bathroom.

"I don't smell that bad," Greg protested.

"It's the combination of all of us." I sprayed the organic orange stuff Grace made us start using three years ago.

Kellen was on his phone, moving away from the group. I raised an eyebrow to Wretch, who shrugged. Greg winked. It seemed his demon senses were as honed as mine.

"So, do you think you can kick my ass now?" Wretch glared at me.

"Yes," I said without hesitation.

"Good."

Greg looked back and forth between us.

Wretch smiled. "I've always known Cim could beat me. Now, he does."

I stared at him. He was serious. Nice to know. I'm sure he'd said something to that effect years ago, but I didn't believe him. I knew it must be true. If you had asked me how I would beat him...well, I didn't know yet.

Kellen rejoined the group. "We're having dinner, Tanith included. It's rare I get to spend time with Cim, but I'm not letting her out of my sight. I'm sure you'd agree."

I did. "If she knows we're keeping an eye on her, she'll rebel."

"She's scared, Cim. This isn't her first experience with demon drugs."

Wretch and Greg raised their hands like kids eager to please the teacher.

"This isn't 'guess the last time'," I said. "I'm sure we all know when she probably was drugged. That doesn't let her off the hook for not checking to make sure I lived."

Kellen coughed. Glancing sideways at him, I saw him fighting a smile. I fought the urge to hit someone. The new powers would take adjustment. If that meant I had a better chance at survival, it would be worth it.

Chapter Ten

Dinner turned into an awkward affair. Tanith sat next to Kellen, talking business. Wretch and I watched the demons two tables over who were faking innocent. Greg drooled over the showgirls. I hoped they didn't have allergies.

Tanith didn't speak to me, although she didn't insult me. That was new.

"Excuse me, gentlemen. I have people to watch." She nodded at each of us individually as she left the table.

Wretch's grin glowed across the room. "The arctic thaw is possible."

"Shut up."

"Cim, she may talk to you yet."

I grumbled something about his shifting dick size while getting up to follow her.

She knew I stood behind her, gesturing to a side office. "Go in, sit down."

"I'm not twelve, Tanith." I stood defiantly, feeling less like a grown dragon and more like a petulant child. She and my mother could do that to me.

"Fine." She slammed the door shut. "Why are you here? I'm fine, go away."

My turn to laugh. "I'm sorry, Princess. Did you think we came for you? Does your ego fill the entire casino or just any room I'm in? Besides, you knew we were coming, so what the fuck is this really about?"

"Fuck you."

"Never again." My body ignored that response. "You're easy."

She was right. "You're deadly."

"You grew."

"You left."

Quietly, almost under her breath, she said, "I was drugged."

"Drugs or not, you tried to scratch my heart out on our wedding day. Why the fuck am I the only one bothered by that?" I was shouting at that point, not caring who heard us.

Her reaction caught me off guard. She sat down, not looking me in the eye. I waited. Silence filled the room. I heard her uneven breathing as she struggled to calm down. Not the reaction I'd expected. I'd played this moment over in my head for decades. Not once did she look apologetic and hurt.

Trying to hide my confusion and compassion for whatever she held inside, I crossed my arms in front of my chest, leaning back against the wall.

"I was drugged. I didn't so much leave you at the altar as I had a horrible drug trip I barely remember."

I wanted to let her off the hook. I did.

I wouldn't. "You know what happened. There's no way it didn't get back to you."

"I know. Your mother described it to me. In minute detail."

She looked up and I swear I saw regret there.

My mother had a gift for guilt. She could make the cardinals at the Vatican feel shame. "You left the country for thirty years."

"It was part of the deal."

That caught my attention. "What deal?"

"Your mother told me if she found me in the states for the next twenty years, she'd rip my head off." She looked up at me, still slightly afraid. "I made it thirty, just in case."

I believed her. My mother protected me for fifty years before I left the family home. What I didn't like was her threatening Tanith without mentioning it to me. Of course, if I'd heard about it, I would've chased my beloved across the world to get her back. "You've continued to ignore me for the last seventy years. Care to blame that on my mother?"

"No. I'm done talking." She left.

I waited. I knew he'd heard the entire thing.

Ten seconds later, Wretch walked in, closing the door behind him. "You believe her?"

"You've met my mother."

He nodded. "That doesn't explain why she didn't contact you for seventy years." He held his hand up to prevent me from speaking. "I'm suspicious, Cim. Where could she have been for thirty years? We didn't hear of her in Europe, or India. Where else could she have gone? I didn't find her in Vegas until after you and Nitha had your pool fight ten years ago."

I knew where he was pushing me. I wouldn't say it.

"She was with Kragen, Cim. Face it. The drug ring we are chasing had to start back then. Maybe Tanith was a voluntary test subject."

This got more twisted every day. "She's not trying to get us involved, Wretch. If Tanith voluntarily helped for thirty years, I'll tear her head off myself. It would explain her not mentioning her boyfriend's drug problem before she got beaten. At least, to Kellen."

Wretch scoffed. "She showed up in your bedroom doorway, Cim."

As she had on the night she'd attacked me? "A century later with the same drug in her wounds? I doubt it."

He clucked his tongue. "Don't be so sure."

"If this trail leads back to Kragen, I owe you. For now, let's concentrate on keeping werewolves from getting addicted. Humans will end up in psychiatric wings for reporting hallucinations. They take quick action when one of theirs loses touch. We have to make sure the wolves and other shifters don't get hooked on the ability to see demons."

Wretch laughed. "What an unexpected side effect."

"If that's the case, the demon population should be going down. What if this was Kragen's plan all along? Obsidian is trying to increase the demon population but they don't get addicted to drugs. For his business to thrive, and to get back at your grandmother, he could use this to remove demon threats around the world. He's never gotten past her hold on Asia. That market would open up for him if he eliminated enough demons to leave her vulnerable."

He stared at me.

I tried to keep the smile to a minimum. "I know the demons have disappeared into the manufacturing plant, not the bottom of Lake Tahoe. I'm thinking outside of the box. You should be proud; you've been poking me to do it for centuries." We both new why I was able to think clearer. It bothered me while being exhilarating.

"Werewolves can see us while drugged. Killing demons before they fully materialize is efficient, smart, and would decimate the population." He sounded a little wistful. "This would be the only way to eliminate my family's power. Other paranormals don't answer to us. Only demons who've learned by reputation that defying Nitha or Obsidian end up in a centuries-long torture session."

Sitting down, I thought it through. If we left this alone, Kragen's drug could have the opposite effect. Could I stay in New Orleans while dragons and shifters removed a huge chunk of the demon population? Yes, I could.

I looked at my best friend of four hundred years. "If we leave this alone, the demon population in the states could drop. That would cripple Obsidian's power. If we let dragons know in Europe, we could destroy her operation worldwide. I have connections to the dragons in Asia. I know that's her home base. They leave her alone because they're afraid of retaliation."

"This eliminates their fear of being overrun in their homes at night." He spoke quietly.

He didn't look well to me. "Are you okay with this?"

He shifted to his demon form. "This doesn't walk across the earth without destroying everything in its path. My mother may have been trying to breed demon out of the population. Maybe blended species stood a chance. Laythe mentioned it a few times but pulled away when I pressed her on it." He shifted back to human dandy. "We cannot commit genocide, Cim. Demons will always exist. However, if we are vulnerable, as we have never been before, we might be forced to get along with other species."

"Innocent demons who despise their heritage will be killed as well, you know this. When wolf packs find out they can take on demons, there will be a frenzy." Payback for centuries of being killed and eaten by demons, werewolf being a delicacy in the paranormal community up until the formation of the Court.

"We've mutilated millions of humans, wolves, and shifters. Humans would avoid harming innocents, Cim. We aren't human." He sounded disappointed.

I was happy not to be human. They smelled funny to me. Wretch was right. Humans looked down on anyone who stayed silent during genocide. The Court would have to be notified. I'd heard a rumor my mother knew the dragons on the Court. She was a good woman. Her moral compass would be challenged by this knowledge. If I didn't tell her, my life would be in danger.

Then she'd demand I pair up with a female to have children. That thought made me shudder.

Which brought me back to Tanith. "I have to talk to her. Alone, when she can't walk away."

"My suite?" He perked up. Kidnapping her from the casino floor got his blood flowing.

"I want to talk to her, not apologize for you." I laughed, though. The mental image of him vanishing with her in the middle of the floor made me very happy.

"You guys in here?" Kellen came in with Greg. "I'm used to a demon-infested Vegas. This doesn't feel right. It smells different. It's better, don't get me wrong; they stink." He looked over at Wretch, hoping he'd smile. "There are six in this entire hotel. Two of them are working out in the hotel gym."

"Distribution," Wretch and I said together.

Kellen sat at the table. "What's happening? It can't be only the drug distribution. Younger demons don't give a shit about territory, heritage, or family loyalty." He turned to Wretch. "You explained it to me like the Mafia. Each demon family has a head, with a few confidants, then they have a few more, until you get to the bottom, correct?"

"Yes." He sounded proud. "The latest generation of demons, those turned off by the violence of my grandmother and her team, denounced the entire set-up. They walked away without repercussions because the population was already low. My grandmother would torture fellow demons, but if she thought there lay a chance she'd use them later, she'd let them live."

Kellen pulled a dry erase marker from his pocket before tapping the wall. A section slid back, revealing a large, white board. "This poker room doubles as one of my offices. I don't stay in one place for long. I change it up every month."

Impressive. My isolation in New Orleans for the past two hundred years kept me from other dragons. Demons liked partying at my club and gambling for human money. Other than Wretch's family, we hadn't had to fight off any real threats.

Kellen was the closest I had to family in the United States. Using human genealogy charts, we would be cousins.

He was drawing a flowchart on the board. At the top, he put Obsidian. Wretch sat as a lone square off to the right. "This is the organization I know about."

Wretch got up and looked it over. "That's about right. Obsidian is the eldest demon, Kragen is second, Vex is third. You put Narran and the kids on here. We killed them." He erased their names with his hand.

"I know. The fewer blanks we have, the better." Kellen put empty squares in the spaces.

I recognized most of the names. None of the top demons came to New Orleans while Laythe was there. She might've been a disappointment to her mother by not torturing humans, and she excelled at terrorizing demons into behaving. Which was why Obsidian beheaded her, in front of us.

That memory wouldn't go away. "Why are you putting marks on some of the demons?"

Kellen drew across fourteen demon names. "They are missing. Either they're in Asia working at Obsidian's places in Thailand, or there's a bigger problem here. Kragen doesn't change his team. Drake is the only one he trusts with his organization. Everyone else, to him, is expendable."

"Are we really worried about the ruin of demons?" Tanith's angry tone made Kellen wince. She stood in the doorway, hands on her hips.

"I don't know. I figure if all of them die off, it would be a good thing." He didn't look at Wretch.

The only demon-dragon hybrid in existence cleared his throat. "I doubt the population would collapse as much as you seem to think. There are millions."

I'd thought it was thousands. I wasn't alone; the silence in the room gave it away.

"Millions of demons?" Greg lowered his head.

I'd never heard a paranormal pray before then. Greg's words sounded unintelligible even though the intent rang clear.

"Can you do that for us, too?" Tanith asked when he finished. "I'd assumed thousands."

"We all did." I distinctly remember Laythe telling me it was less than five thousand. The difference was so large it couldn't have been accidental. At that moment, our concern lay with the drugs. "We need to find their local warehouse and shut it down."

Kellen stared at Tanith, hard. "Talk."

She stood straighter. "What makes you think I know?"

He didn't flinch. I liked him more. "You know."

Resignation bent her shoulders forward. "I know where he picked up the supply, if that's what you mean."

Alluding to her boyfriend that way, without any pain in her voice for the missing man, made me happy. It shouldn't have. It did. No wonder my mother and Wretch had kept her location secret.

"Tell us where it is. We'll go shut it down." Wretch stood, rolling his shoulders back. In seconds, he'd transformed into a form I hadn't seen in a hundred years.

A demon in a suit. Horns rose two inches above his skull; blackest black hair fell to his waist in waves. He'd bulked up his muscles, making them visible when he moved. The vertical slits in his yellow eyes warned every paranormal to back away. Wretch's reputation had been built in this form. His portrait had become the epitome of demon and devil folklore. The brutality in those stories hadn't been exaggerated.

"Can we fly there?" I wanted to arrive in dragon form. Gunfire from guards would bounce from my scales.

Tanith shook her head. "Even after dark, the warehouse is lit up. It's only two blocks from the strip."

I understood. "Less suspicious than a lone warehouse in the middle of desert."

Kellen nodded. "I'm going with you. Tanith, the casino is yours."

She opened her mouth to protest, stopping as she thought about it. "You're right. I wouldn't be any good."

Greg stood up, sighing.

I followed him out the door. "You okay with this?"

"Yes." The look in his eyes showed the same doubts I had.

"If you don't think you can handle it, I need to know now." I'd not push him away—he had to choose.

"I know what addiction feels like, Cim. No one deserves to have the horrors inflicted by a dependent mind slipped in silently." Determination fixed his jaw in place. "Even if we remove thousands of demons, the addicts would self-destruct. It could decimate the shifter population."

Good, his head was in the right space.

"Agreed." I'd seen the affliction of alcoholism on humans. A brutal, horrendous disease leaving almost-corpses shaking for days as they tried to break free.

Tanith headed to the casino floor. All I saw was her rigid back. I opened my mouth to find the words in my head which proved too jumbled to assemble into a coherent sentence.

"Dammit." The best I could do.

"Shakespeare, bug up your ass?" Wretch joined me.

"Shut up."

"She still does it for you."

It had bothered him before. "You have a problem with that?"

He snorted in feigned offense. "You're a dragon. You do what you want." He still looked like a demon.

"You planning on walking around like that?" He would terrify humans.

"Absolutely. This is Vegas. Chicks dig a great costume."

"Until they realize the mask doesn't come off." We'd seen that scenario play out before.

"No touching human women, Wretch," Kellen admonished him as he closed the room. "We have enough to deal with. I'm not going to lose manpower in damage control."

"You two are killing my patrolling buzz." He shifted back to demon dandy. A few more gold necklaces than usual, but that fit Vegas.

Chapter Eleven

Greg stood close, silently scanning everyone who walked by. "I can see demons."

"And dead people. Don't forget to say dead people," Wretch teased.

"No, Wretch. I can see demons walking by in the ether." His face looked ashen.

"What did you drink today?" I turned him towards me.

He didn't look drugged.

"Since we landed, what you gave me." He stared at Wretch.

My hybrid friend had a complete internal fit of fury with only his eyes giving it away. "They spiked the drinks in my suites?"

Kellen was already on the phone, yelling at someone. "I don't care who said what. You clear all of the bottles out of his rooms. *Now.* Then you report to me, personally. I want to see your face when you lie to me."

"Cim, I'm okay. I don't feel drugged at all. There's no loss of sensation or change in my head other than seeing demons walking. It's disturbing." He shook his head like it would make the sand-shaking noise and go away.

"If I hear rattling, you want me to cut it off?" Wretch shifted an arm into a sword shape.

"Disco killer," Kellen said, laughing. "I can't see them. So I'm still in the clear."

"Tanith," I said, knowing.

She stood in the middle of the casino floor as we approached, looking at a wall with a mural painted on it.

"Greg?"

"Yeah, demons are flowing through the wall like a hose has been turned up." He stepped beside me. "They're nodding at her as they walk past. At least, they're not acknowledging me."

"They will," Wretch said, speaking the spell for communication. "As soon as they know you can see them, an alert will go up and you will be marked as a threat in the demon world. Right now, you're an amusement, a wolf with a taste of what full-blooded demons get at birth. This will get ugly."

Greg stepped slightly backwards, keeping Wretch and myself between him and the line of demons. That's when I realized I'd been seeing them all along.

"Wretch?"

"I figured if Wolf Boy could see them, so could you." He stared ahead as he spoke. "This is too many in one area. The magic level will be off-the-charts bad."

"Too high for what?"

I kept the worry from my voice. The one ability I'd wanted was vanishing and reappearing. Now, I could shift with a thought. If there existed too much magic in the area and I decided I wanted to be somewhere else? Fuck.

"It won't short anything out," he said, making direct eye contact with a number of the wanderers. "Laythe warned me that too much magic in one area could set off a chain reaction if anyone was unstable. This kind of energy attracts psychotic demons by the dozens."

"Or on drugs?" Greg's voice gave away his fear.

"The drug doesn't affect us, as far as we know. That should keep the danger down. Seems there's a side effect to the manufacturing process." Wretch waved at one woman while she walked through as if pulled unwillingly.

"She's not happy," Greg said, and I nodded in agreement.

"I'll tell you her story some time. Not now." Wretch waved his hand and Tanith spun around. "I removed her ability to see them."

She blinked, turned back to the line that still flowed through the room, and came over to us. "I'd rather see them, Demon, than know they are there and be blind to their presence."

"As you wish," he said, ducking as she swung at him.

"Why can I see them?" Tanith shivered.

"Exposure to the drug. Are there any of your boyfriend's bodily fluids in your system?" Wretch asked then stepped away from her and me.

Tears formed in her eyes. "He can see this?"

"If he's still alive," I answered, feigning concern.

"He's not the only one, I'm sure." Even she knew that sounded lame.

"Billy," Greg said, reminding me of Grace's boyfriend. "If he can see this…"

I'd never met the boy and had no idea how he'd take it. Grace never dated men who couldn't handle Wretch and I on our best days.

I'd bet he was dead in New Orleans. "I doubt he's alive."

We walked back to Kellen's 'sometime' office. He stood in the door. "You have a call."

I never turned my phone on. Picking up the extension he pointed me to, I heard Grace's angry breathing before she started in on me. "Some days, I fucking hate you."

"Glad to hear you're okay."

"Billy's dead."

"Grace—"

"Don't. They dropped his body off in front of the club. George brought him inside. Angie says he's full of the drug she found in Tanith. She's doing the autopsy in your basement. Drake Kane dropped by to see you. Cim, he's slick and as trustworthy as a drunken snake oil salesman. He gave me his card and his personal number. I wanted to cough a hairball onto his thousand-dollar shoes." Her voice broke only once.

"You barf on Drake any time you want. Sorry about Billy. We're going to finish up here by tomorrow night. With them dropping him at our door, I don't want to be gone longer than that. Stay at the house in my room tonight. George snores loud enough to rattle the light fixtures but he jumps up if a mouse farts. Also, Elise works with and sleeps with Kane. If she comes by, pretend you don't know."

Her laughter let me know she'd be okay. Before George joined our group, I would've flown back immediately.

Wretch raised an eyebrow at me when I returned.

"Billy's dead. They dropped him at our doorstep. Same drug." I nodded at Tanith. "Angie's on it."

Tanith coughed, excused herself, and left. Kellen started after her.

"She's realized her boyfriend is probably dead. Let her go."

If he was alive in that warehouse, but barely, this made his mercy killing easier.

Greg kept staring at the wall like he expected a line of demons to wander through. "When do we blow up the warehouse? It's like it's calling them home."

Wretch's head popped up so fast I thought he'd shifted. "A beacon." Then, he vanished.

This time, it was Greg who said, "I hate it when he does that."

"We'll go up the slow way. He'll have it figured out by the time we get there."

"I'm coming," Kellen said, erasing the board. He closed up the room as we waited.

The walk to the elevators wove around the line of demons. Any skepticism I'd had about the beacon theory dissipated as I watched them walk trance-like through the hotel.

The door to the suite lay open. Wretch paced on the second-floor stair landing. He'd shifted into a dragon with demon horns and hooves.

"That's a form I haven't seen before," Greg said, heading for the kitchenette. It'd been too long between meals for all of us.

I walked over to the two-story high windows. Below me trailed a wispy blue line of demons heading away from the strip. I could see a faint trace in the distance. "Well, we don't have to search for the warehouse. Seems we can follow the zombie demons."

"Not funny," Wretch said, looking worried.

Knowing that when Wretch worried, the world started to tilt into darkness, I sent text messages to Grace and George, asking them to stay in tonight and keep Angie there with them.

Greg returned with the smell of steak on him. "Food?" Wretch perked up.

"We all need to eat. I want to talk to Dale in case the blowback gets home before we do," Greg said.

Hearing steaks sizzle on the countertop grill halted my train of thought. "You brought steak?"

"It was in the fridge, enough for all four of us. I just turned the grill on." He walked back to the kitchen.

Wretch laughed. "I called ahead."

I didn't think that far ahead. "Nice."

"We were bringing a werewolf to Vegas. I asked for a cow." He flipped up his shirt collar.

"Kellen, you're welcome to join us for dinner. It appears we have enough food." Dragons will eat anything.

Wretch waved us around the corner to the dining room. I loved this suite—a luxury condo with three bedrooms and enough space to house us without stumbling over each other. For a flying man, I preferred the top floors. I could jump out of a window and catch air before going splat.

Out of habit, I filled the water glasses from the pitcher Greg brought over. Wretch had shooed him out of the kitchen. I could hear meat sizzling and hunger pushed aside all of my earlier concerns.

He wasn't kidding about the cow. We each had a one-inch thick steak and a large baked potato. No need for salad. I'd never eaten it, only pushed it around on my plate. It took two trips for more beer to wash the meal down.

When we finished, I cleaned up. Greg pulled Kellen aside as we moved back to the living room. I fought the urge to follow.

Wretch stood next to me with his head tilted. "How much can we trust him?"

"Greg?"

"Kellen." He elbowed me. "Greg's covered our asses a couple of times now. He's good."

"If you weren't by my side, Kellen would be."

Kellen had proved a great asset. His talents at finding demons trying to get one over on humans were so good, he had the whole strip to himself. Before he took over, there'd been two dragons situated on either end.

The other two returned.

Kellen spoke first. "I'm going to stay here while you go to the warehouse. Remember, other than an odd alley or two, there are cameras watching at all times. It's why the demons distribute by appearing inside places they control. You won't see them walking the streets here. Our demon employees, one hundred at last count, have a special room for arrivals and departures after their shifts. It's a great system."

I went back to the window, spying the line of demons still moving. "That's wrong. Everything about it screams set up."

Wretch and Greg joined me.

My friend agreed. "It does. I've never seen this before."

This bothered me. I noticed the wolf rubbed his face, trying to hide his concern, as well. "Greg, it's okay to let us know you're worried."

"I'm worried about home. The pack doesn't have the ability to see this. If there's one back home…"

I picked up his train of thought. "We are in deep shit. Tell him there are a few demons we trust to point any recent odd behavior. He can call Grace for the list. They'll tell her and George at the club so it won't look suspicious."

He nodded before texting his alpha.

"We need to check out the warehouse. I want to know what it looks like," Wretch said.

No need for an address when we could follow the line. As we passed through the casino, Kellen waved. I wanted him to know what time we'd left. Tanith pretended she didn't see us. Greg thought it amusing. He'd learn.

Once outside, the heat proved oppressive. It felt like the sun sat on the roofs of the buildings. Wretch gave all of us stylish sunglasses. I appreciated it.

The line of demons went straight down Las Vegas Boulevard onto Mandalay Bay Road. We pretended we belonged as we walked over the highway bridge. Off to our left, we could see them enter a low-lying building surrounded by portable storage units that had been dropped on sand. A few dumpsters littered the area. It sat between the roads and exit ramp.

The line of demons walked right through the front door.

"That's convenient," Greg said, stopping to smell the air. "Demons and shifters."

Wretch seemed confused. "In the middle of a space? Who the hell was running this thing? My demon side is offended by the lack of planning."

I felt like a recording. "It's a trap or a decoy."

"Yes, but that doesn't mean it's okay to be lazy about it." He walked off, angry.

"His demon side?" Greg was concerned.

"Sloppiness pisses him off. He's killed demons for having stupid plans, or bad execution. His family does carry out their plans with precision." I liked that about Wretch.

"A demon purist who hates demons?" Greg put a hand on my back, nudging me along. "We have company."

I looked at the line we'd followed. "A lot of it."

"No. Live, rotting human body company," he said, wrinkling his nose.

The smell hit me as he spoke.

Wretch walked around a storage unit. "Well, how are you doing?"

A struggled cry erupted before the sounds of a fight.

Following the noise, we found Wretch with an angry demon soul floating over his head, cursing. The human body lay crumpled on the ground.

"Human soul?" I asked.

"Relieved and gone." He stood poking the demon soul with a rib bone. "Tell me what is going on here and we'll see about finding you a new body to take over. Only this time, a demon one."

The swirling, foul green mess bobbed up and down in the air.

"Is that thing jumping for joy?" Greg put a hand over his nose.

"The only thing more important to a demon than torturing human beings is immortality," I explained.

Greg nodded his understanding. Then he began to look confused." How do we talk to a disembodied demon soul?"

"That's why we have Wretch."

Being able to use his demon abilities to destroy other demons made him happy. He shifted into his demon form, grabbing the soul with two hands. In the four hundred years I'd been killing and devouring demon souls, I had never spent this much time in the presence of one. The smell was a disgusting combination of landfill, swamp, and decaying flesh. The conversation sounded unintelligible. However, I could feel the communication. Like a wire running through me attuned to the magic they were using. One glance over at Greg and it was clear he felt it, too.

"Please tell me this isn't normal," the concerned werewolf asked.

I shook my head in the negative. Wretch shoved the vile soul away from him reflexively. He then waved his right hand, outlining the infinity symbol in the air. I had only seen him do this once before. It activated a condemnation spell, banning the soul to the ether for all eternity. It appeared he wasn't going to be any help, after all. The soul vanished from visible space but was immediately visible in the same strange blue light as the line we had been following.

Stepping around the storage container, I saw the end of the string of demons. The last thing that could be glimpsed as it vanished into the warehouse was the soul Wretch had banished. A fresh breeze helped clear the air. I heard Greg inhaling deeply.

"I'm not sure I will ever get used to the smell of demon souls," he said.

Wretch shifted back into his demon dandy form. "The little shit didn't know anything. He bragged about working for Kragen against my grandmother. He was quite surprised to find out that I considered it a smart move."

"You banished him for eternity even though you support his decision?" My tone came out sarcastic but I wanted an answer.

He smiled at me, displaying demon teeth. "He was so offended, he decided to insult my friends. No one does that."

Greg stood little taller and rolled his shoulders back like he'd gotten a compliment from the king of the world. I had to smile.

The bile smell reached my nose. Turning my way head away from the stench, I heard the unmistakable sound of a human throwing up. Wretch immediately straightened his collar and ran his fingers through his hair. Clearly, he'd assumed we'd found a damsel in distress. Greg stifled a laugh next to me. Whoever it was didn't need all three of us watching them throw up.

"Devil!"

Terrified human screams hit a pitch that made me grit my teeth. From the grimace on Greg's face, I'm guessing he had the same reaction. Since we'd be found in a moment, we stepped out from behind the building. Wretch sauntered back to us with a sarcastic grin lighting his face. Behind him, a beautiful human woman ran towards the highway with her long brown hair flowing behind her.

"I see you made an impression."

He smiled. "Some women don't appreciate all of my forms."

Greg laughed. He was wise enough not to say anything, though.

Chapter Twelve

The warehouse stood a couple hundred yards away. Three werewolf guards wandered in our direction. If that was the reaction to a woman screaming, this might be a very good day for us. I glanced over at Greg who shook his head 'no' at the unspoken question. He didn't know them.

Spotting something in the distance, they took off at a run. Turning quickly to check what got their attention, I saw the human woman standing on the edge of the highway trying to flag down a ride. Seemed she may need our rescue, after all. I held up my hand to prevent Wretch from moving.

I looked at Greg and pointed in the woman's direction. "You go. They might leave her be if they think she's being picked up by another wolf."

His new abilities got him to her quick enough to calm her down. When the guards arrived, Greg pulled her in for a tight hug. It appeared they were going to leave her alone when someone else stepped out of the warehouse door.

Clearly the demon in charge. She'd chosen a human form with Asian features, much like Obsidian. She vanished from where she stood and instantly appeared next to the werewolves at the road.

"If you had let me go get her, she'd be standing here with us now instead of holding on to Greg for dear life." Wretch tried to sound humble.

"Feel free to pop on over there and check things out," I said to his vanishing form.

I watched the animated discussion, knowing who would win ahead of time, because my friends cheated. I had to wonder why they wanted this woman back. Was she one of their test subjects? If they were using humans as guinea pigs for Red Lady, the Court wouldn't say anything if we decided to burn the whole thing to the ground. Which, given all the smells and the sounds coming from the open door, sounded like a good idea. We would have to plan it carefully, though, since we were out in the open.

Exposure made the Court angrier than breaking any of the written rules. Even if one of their members caused it. My stomach leapt at the horrendous odors wafting my way.

How did werewolves work around this? Their senses were better than mine. As I watched the demon woman, Wretch and the human vanished. Greg ran back to me while the other wolves looked confused.

"I'm guessing that didn't go well?"

"You could say that." He paused as we watched the other wolves make their way back to the warehouse. "She's the demon in charge, reports straight to Kragen."

"Are they using humans as lab rats?" I knew the answer.

"It sure looks that way. She tried to convince us that sacrificing a few humans was worth the price. She didn't specify why, though. When Wretch pushed her on it, they vanished."

"Did Wretch go voluntarily?"

He looked scared. "I don't think so."

Greg and I made our way to the back of the building. We found windows on this side. Demons and wolves paced on elevated walkways. Even with our hearing, the conversations sounded muted. We stood near three trash dumpsters. Fluids leaked from the bottom, filling the air with the smell of death and decay. Now I understood the placement of the building. Car exhausts, especially diesel ones, would cover some of the stench.

The two of us stood there with our shirts over our noses, hoping for a thunderous downpour. No clouds could be seen for miles.

"Let's try the other side." I walked backwards until the wind changed, giving us relief.

"What the hell is that stench?" Greg dry heaved.

"Dead bodies. I know where they are getting their drugs." One of the most gruesome ways to create drugs. The stuff is injected into the victim's body, time is allowed for their system to react, and then their blood is extracted. Given the amount of blood and stench coming from the waste, they were killing the human subjects and dumping them.

Red Lady must start as cocaine and demon magic injected into humans. After extraction, it was likely dehydrated, then sold, or added to drinks and supplements.

Not only would that be enough to have somebody's magic removed, Kragen and every ranking member of his organization could be killed. An extermination process I'd insist Wretch and I carry out.

Demon and dragon species had existed for thousands of years before humanity evolved, and yet, without humans, we'd be living in caves and forests.

"How many trash bins do you see?" I raised an eyebrow.

Greg stood from his bent position. "There's two behind you. One more on the south side of the warehouse, up against the adjoining building."

Glancing out, I saw another bin. Red liquid leaked from the rusted-out corners. "Blood."

Wretch appeared on the roof of the warehouse. There must likely be vents up there to keep it cooler in the desert sun. He wandered around until we lost him behind the roof access door.

"I didn't see that." My powers of observation helped keep us alive and I'd missed it. Tanith in my life, even tangentially, screwed up my scouting.

"I did. Too busy gagging to point out." Greg's breath still ragged, reeking of bile. "There are so many wrong smells here. Either the shifters are drugged to ignore it, or that building has an amazing air freshener system. It would keep any curious noses far away. With a good breeze, they could clear out blocks of us without any further effort."

"Genius." Disgusting as it was, I had to admit the tactic proved a good one.

He moved behind me to lean on the brick wall shading us. "Yes."

"Any ideas?"

"Wait for Wretch," he said, holding his breath.

"You're a great help," I teased. "He may look free, but he didn't go in under his own power. He'd be next to us. We have to get him out."

"Shut up."

Shouts came from inside. "We have no idea what we're going to run into, but I'll go first in case they start shooting. My scales can take a bullet."

"Let me shift," he said.

A group of human pedestrians walked within earshot. I started to pace.

"You'd be a horrible wolf."

I turned my head away. "I'm impatient."

He hadn't moved. "Exactly."

"Good thing I can fly."

"Especially now that humans can shoot things in the air."

"Fuck you." I laughed.

He held up a hand. Something had changed. "There's a new odor. Perfumey." He crinkled his nose.

"Air freshener?"

"Human perfume."

A couple wandered to the back parking lot. He was a werewolf; she bathed in the kind of perfume teenagers hosed people with at the entrance to department stores. My turn to gag. "Either she's elderly and it's being hidden by a demon spell…"

"Or a demon luring a wolf." Greg leapt behind another building. Hidden in the shadows, he watched as they came our way.

"I'll take her. You get him," I said, taking a deep breath of perfume. Better than bile, though.

Greg nodded, his eyes already shifted.

I extended the claws on both hands, ready to change should it go wrong. I knew it would the closer they came.

The demon woman shifted into Wretch. "Greg, this guy was in a cage. They're using wolves as lab rats in there." He vanished again.

Greg took the stunned wolf's hand, pulling him into the alley with us.

"Who the fuck are you?" He tried to fight.

"Greg. I'm with the New Orleans pack. This is Cimmerian; you'll know him as Death Dealer. Your rescuer is Wretch." Greg wrapped both arms around the struggling man, squeezing the fight out of him.

"Let me go." He started to shift.

If he changed into wolf, we'd never find him again, and I needed answers. One swipe across his face with my claws calmed him. He remained human.

I shifted to keep him that way. "We pulled your mangy ass out of there. Who's running this, where do we find them, and how many more trips does my friend have to make to save everyone?" My voice trembled with anger, lowered for full effect.

"Ten." His voice squeaked. He coughed. "Ten wolves in cages. They killed the rest. You can smell them from here." His eyes watered. "My mate was one of them. There are fifty humans. The ones who are still alive want to be killed."

Greg's grip loosened as the man hunched forward. "Sorry to hear that. We'll get the rest out. Don't tell anyone we were here."

"This place has to be shut down, and you want me to be quiet?"

I shifted back to human, clothing myself with demon magic. "No, you don't have to be quiet. In fact, announce it. Just keep our names out of it."

"I'll wait until the rest of my pack is free." He crossed his arms, trying to look less scared than he smelled.

"Your choice."

Wretch appeared five feet from us with a wolf on each arm. Their clothing hung in tattered shreds, exposing oozing wounds with matted fur. Greg sprinted to them, lifting them with care as Wretch vanished again. Three safe; eight more to go. This would take a while. I planned on going to get the humans out as soon as Wretch was done. His blood would power the drugs better than any shifter. If I'd figured that out, so did Kragen. I hoped the woman running this place wouldn't find him as he popped in and out.

"Greg, stay with them. I'll get food." The closest fast food place was less than a block away. I followed the smell, running behind buildings. I ate two full meals myself while they filled my huge order. Enough hamburgers for each wolf to get two and fries, and bottles of water from a drug store on the way back.

The food scent wafted around the corner before I did. Greg sprinted out to grab the bags from me before the others tore me apart. He left the food in a pile, stepping back. They looked rabid as they inhaled it all. I counted eleven wolves.

"Wretch?" I caught Greg's gaze across the *mêlée*.

"One last trip." He shrugged.

An explosion ripped through the air. I took off running toward the fireball after seeing Greg leading the wolves toward a side street. A scream caught my attention. Running from the demons streaming toward me, I veered in the direction of the sound. Rare to hear that sound without Wretch on the receiving end.

I rounded the corner away from the dumpster and there they stood, he in demon form, a smiling mouth splitting his head in half as he chuckled. In front of him was a demon female, ranting about lost revenue. He wasn't fazed, waving me off.

"The rats abandoning ship are headed this way. Either kill her or throw her at them," I said, shifting.

We found ourselves far enough from the road that we couldn't be seen behind this building unless we flew. It sounded like a zombie movie cast came toward us.

"Are these demons on the drug?"

Her head swiveled around, leaving her neck facing forward. "We all have added abilities now, Death Dealer," she screeched.

My self-preservation instinct shouted for me to get away, even fly over armed humans, to avoid this demon. "Are you the bitch who beat my ex-fiancée so hard she came to me for help?"

"Of course, Death Dealer. How else would we get your and the mutt's blood for our operation?" Her confidence shook me. This was a trap she hadn't sprung yet.

Chuckling, Wretch added, "We're here to chat with you about your operation. I've pulled the wolves out. The humans you sacrificed, I burned out of mercy."

"I lured you here. Today, you die." She turned her head sideways while her bones snapped.

One of the creepiest things I'd seen. Her ribs poked her skin as she rearranged herself. I didn't know what she'd end up being; only that Wretch would get the honor. Her backup horde arrived on cue.

"Cim." He kicked a pile at his feet. Tanith's boyfriend.

"She's going to kill us when we get home." I checked for a pulse. His heart struggled to beat. As I pulled him behind me, I saw injection marks on his arms.

"Fight us," the leader of the shifting horde shouted.

"Who's first?" I asked, stepping forward and shifting to dragon, leaving the demon spikes on. I'd need them to survive zombie demons.

"All of us," he answered as they lurched en masse.

Stretching my hands, I shifted longer claws. Each neck I saw, I slashed. The leader hit me in the stomach with a piece of metal. I turned to see clear liquid dripping from it.

"If you're trying to drug me, you don't know me." I grabbed the demon trying to pull my wing off by the head. Twisting until it snapped, I pulled his spine out to see his cowering soul clinging to the vertebrae. "You look tasty," I said, drinking in.

The group gasped. Hearing about my reputation was one thing; seeing me was even better. I slowed down my movements to make sure they caught every second of the show.

"That looked good. Mind if I join in?" Greg shifted his jaws only, keeping his massive size.

I gestured him to the back of the group.

The leader thrust his metal stick at my left wing. I pulled it behind my body, grabbing a trembling demon in front of me. With the next thrust, I pushed the demon in the way. He began to gurgle while melting. Yuck, a demon puddle at me feet. His soul was gone.

"You will no longer be a threat to us. We can die without leaving our souls vulnerable," the female demon announced with pride.

"Very strong words for a woman in your position," I said.

Wretch dangled her by her ankles. "She's feisty. I like it."

"Ah, hell." I laughed.

Greg chuckled next to me.

"You got to the front way too easy." Demons scattered behind him.

"I know. Let's take it as a win for now. Who's the moaning lump?" He shifted back to human.

"Tanith's boyfriend," I said, heading over to the young man. His pulse faded beneath my fingers. "She's going to blame me for this."

"We can bring this bitch back to the casino. I'm sure the five of us can peel her apart." Lowering his voice, Wretch spoke a spell and the demon snapped back to human form.

"My work is done," she announced, trying to shift. "Fuck, what did you do?"

"You're human now." He morphed back to demon dandy, dropping her on her head.

"Vicious fucking cunt, I'll kill you," Tanith screamed behind me, running at full speed.

I politely stepped out of the way, pulling a stunned Greg with me.

"She didn't stay at the hotel." He smiled at me.

"Listening to us is not one of her skills," I filled in.

Kellen walked up next. "Mine, either."

"Now I know why the horde left early."

"We peeled off a few who'd decided to skip the fighting." My fellow dragon grinned, his shifted canines showing.

Wretch handed the female demon to Tanith. "I'm not sure she's the one who hurt him, girl, but she gave the orders," he said, stepping back.

The demon shouted a spell and the demon ghost line popped out of the wall behind her. Instead of staying blue and ethereal, they snapped into existence, filling the air with decaying demon stench and growls.

"We're fucked," Greg said, shifting.

"As usual," I agreed.

"New accessories." The wolf noted my spikes. "Those should help."

He shifted into a full wolf while Kellen changed into a sand-colored dragon. From the air, he'd blend into the desert.

There was tugging at my back. Turning my head, I couldn't see what it was. I focused, popping the demon spikes out farther, and was awarded with a thud. Down at my ankles scrambled half a demon. The top half ran on its hands toward the female leader.

"I'm in a bad horror movie," I said.

"We all will be if we don't get out of here. We're winning too easily." Kellen swung his tail, taking five demons out. No souls left writhing; just goo on the ground.

"That's wrong," Greg said.

In front of me stood a large demon growing his arms long enough to reach his toes. Missing his throat, I swiped his collarbone, scraping it. He wrapped his arms around me, encompassed my wings. I was in trouble. Behind me, the sound of a sword being drawn from a steel scabbard had me worried. I felt a blow to my back, like I'd been hit on a scar, the sound metal on metal. The face in front of me grinned.

Twisting in the hold, I extended my talons, clawing at my captor's arms. He healed as fast as I cut. I leaned back and felt his feet barely leave the ground. Smiling, I fell over onto my back, pulling him with me. A blade passed through his back, stopping at my scales. He wasn't bleeding. How long had he been in the ether? Demons' blood was thick and flowed slowly.

"They don't bleed." I looked over at Wretch.

He had the demon female in the air, trying to get her to give up Kragen's location. She focused on removing the half demon body clinging to her legs.

"There's something wrong with that," Greg coughed. He stood in the middle of two demons, half his height, trying to push him over.

"Yours aren't fighting." I tried to sound happy about it.

"I'm thinking they're stoned. Whatever they took, it's kept them occupied trying to push over the 'furry tree'." He laughed.

The ones attacking me heard a noise I didn't.

"What?" I asked.

"We've been called off," the arms' demon stated. "Have a good day."

They vanished back into the ether, followed by the half-demon. This left us back with the female demon and the knowledge something must be very fucking wrong.

"Wretch, any idea who she is?" I asked. "Greg, run over and see how much of the warehouse is left. If the Court is going to act, especially on one of their own, we need direct proof."

He took off running.

The look on Wretch's face worried me. In four hundred years of friendship, I'd never seen it before.

He started explaining quietly. "The mixture of human blood and demon magic is intoxicating. Adding cocaine made it more addictive. I've hit her a dozen times without being noticed. This is the high demons used to get by drinking human blood."

"Vampire?" I hoped I was joking.

"Where do you think the legend started?" He didn't even look up, mesmerized by her lack of reactions.

I'd assumed some demons pretended to be vampires from time to time, keeping the legend alive. First time I'd heard this version.

"I found this," Greg said, handing me an address book, the edges ragged from flames.

I opened it to find lists of people who'd ordered the drugs. Kragen's name had five stars next to it.

"Fire trucks." Wretch grabbed the female demon. "We need to get back to the loft."

"You're bringing her?" I didn't trust her.

"No, I'll drop her in the middle of the cops. She deserves to sober up in a human jail," he said, vanishing.

Looking around, I saw Tanith cradling the body of her lover in her arms. Kellen stood over them in dragon form.

"We need to vacate." I stared at him, not her.

"I'm bringing him along." Her tone came out defiant. Lifting him up with little effort, she walked to us.

Kellen shifted. I spelled him clothing to cover his human form. Wretch appeared, shifting to his normal human form.

"You didn't kill her," she said to Wretch. An accusation.

He put his hand on her boyfriend, saying, "She'll keep in jail. Your man is dying. We can't save him."

Waving at me, he vanished, taking Tanith and her boyfriend with him.

"I guess we walk," Kellen smirked, starting toward the hotel.

Greg and I followed close behind. Skirting the edge of the buildings, we caught the scent of vomit. The firemen had found the bodies in the dumpsters. Wretch's burning job on the ones still in the warehouse would leave their bones intact so their families could be notified.

Chapter Thirteen

I went over the new information in my mind. Kragen was behind the operation. He used human blood when they had cocaine in their system, extracting it. Then, he could add whatever demon glamour spell he wanted, since all demon spells worked on human blood. The trick would be drying it out so he could add it to other things.

"There are more warehouses," I said to Kellen as we entered the elevator. "He has to have places to dry the blood into powder form."

"We only knew of that one," he said, dialing his phone. "Find out who sold Kragen the warehouse currently attracting all of the attention. Then find out who owns the land. I need this today."

"You have people?" Greg asked, amused.

Kellen nodded. "Dragons have had people for centuries."

We shared a smile. Our knack for bedding the spouses of powerful men got both of us information a few centuries ago when we all lived on the east coast. At one point, we'd challenged each other. We lost by dozens to Wretch. Kellen looked like a Viking god and losing women to a half-demon pissed him off—the start of their rift.

Before the elevator doors opened to our floor, his phone beeped.

"There's one more warehouse owned by the same person, Luke Gentry. I've heard his name before around the casino. A whale with more money than sense." Kellen turned his phone off as we approached Wretch and Tanith.

She had him pinned to the living room floor. Both were in human form. The place looked like a mess.

"Is there something I should know?" I asked, staring at my best friend.

"Don't you fucking dare ask me that! I would never sleep with this harpy." The last words came out as a squeak when she tightened her grip around his neck.

I turned to her. "I know he's a horrendous pain in the ass, but if you kill him, I'll come after you."

Her head spun so fast, her hair fanned out, covering Wretch in gorgeous red waves.

"Tanith, you're drugged. Let him go." I tried to sound calm, but after seeing the zombie state of demons, I knew where this could go for her.

"I hear your heartbeat, demon." She spat on Wretch.

He popped up, turned her around, and pulled her arms behind her back while shouting the spell to keep her human. It seemed he'd waited for us before fighting back. A good idea, since I would've killed him had I seen him on top first.

Kellen stepped forward, leaning as close to her face as he could. "You're not going crazy. You have the drug in you. If you want to know about suddenly experiencing demon powers, talk to Cim or Greg."

Her expression shifted as she turned to me. "Talk."

Keeping her in the dark about my transformation no longer benefited me. "I gain demon powers with each soul I ingest. Heightened senses are part of the package. Greg here was injected with demon DNA as a teen. He has the extra abilities, as well."

Wretch relaxed his grip so she could move a little, keeping the spell active. A rampaging female dragon could rip this place, and us, apart with ease.

"My head is full of sounds. It's loud. The smells…oh God, you need to wash up."

"I've been busy," Wretch replied.

"Not just you, you special idiot. All of you. The smell of death is sickening." She gagged.

Wretch and she disappeared to be replaced by the sounds of vomiting from my bedroom.

"I hope they made it to the bathroom," I said.

Greg and Kellen stared at me. "What?"

"You can't leave her in Vegas with me," the pale dragon said. "I'm not familiar with the changes she'll experience."

The truth hung in the air like a fog choking off any argument my brain rushed to find. "Fuck."

"Boss, she can have my room." Greg tried not to laugh.

"Listen, she's not moving in with me. I agree about keeping her informed, but that doesn't mean she has to live in New Orleans."

"Under your protection, away from Obsidian. She's vulnerable, Cim." Kellen wasn't enjoying this conversation any more than I was.

"Kragen isn't banished. The new demon lord, Luke, won't even live there."

"Did you say Luke?" He stared at me like I'd left my brain on the stove for a week.

"Yes." I was irritated.

"The same Luke who owned the warehouse? If he hears about it, and he will, your people at home are in danger." Kellen grabbed his phone. "Get me a limo for the airport, now."

Greg's face told me he'd added it up, as well. We fell into the trap. Now, we were fair game for his demons.

I called the club; George answered. "We blew up the warehouse. It belonged to the new local demon lord, Luke. There might be repercussions."

His voice caught. "Angie's missing again. Grace locked me in the freezer to go find her."

I hung up while shifting. Flying to the second floor, I found Tanith and Wretch seated on my bed.

"We have to go now. Angie's missing, Grace is on the hunt."

My bag sat unpacked. Picking it up, I turned to see Tanith looking more frightened than ever. Wretch, however, grinned and vanished.

"Fucking prick." Her voice sounded barely audible even with my new enhanced hearing.

"That won't ever change."

She looked up at me. "I know that now. I'm going with you. I've heard Grace is a good person, and Angie. Wretch is really in love."

"Yeah, fucked up my mind, too," I said.

Wretch popped back up. "Tan, we need to get your things now." He gently took her by the hand and vanished.

Shocked didn't even come close to describing how I felt. No time to think, though. We had to go. I spelled clothing for myself and walked to the stairs. Down in the living room stood Kellen and Greg with his bags in his hands.

"The limo is at the Sky Suites back door. I'll fly down tonight." My dragon friend grasped my shoulder. "You'll find them. We'll find them."

Packed into the limo with another dragon, Greg, and Wretch, I fought to keep my worry down. Grace could track a mouse across town; she would find Angie if she was still around.

The plane stood where we'd left it, empty except for a thank-you note from Kragen. "*We found your crew. They were delicious.*"

Wretch ripped it into bits and took the pilot's seat himself.

"He can fly?" Tanith sat down, looking for seat belts.

I laughed. "Yes, demons can't get across oceans without a plane, and pilots for paranormals are hard to find."

Greg found the seat belt she looked for, helping Tanith buckle in. "He might lose Angie and the stewardess in one day?"

I took a moment to remember the feisty Irene who gave as good as Wretch. "Yeah, that'll make him angry."

Greg's head popped up from his phone. "Let's hope he lands first."

"The Wretch you've seen, even in fights, is well under control," I explained.

The information sank in slowly until Tanith spoke up. "He's more dangerous…"

I nodded. "When out of control, he can decimate a room full of elder demons. Obsidian, Vex, and Kragen know this. I'm betting his henchman, Drake Kane, or the new local demon lord, Luke, don't. Otherwise, they wouldn't have gone after Angie."

"Can we have a moment?" Tanith asked.

Greg excused himself. Moments later, I heard water running in the back bedroom. We all needed a shower.

Tanith's internal temper tantrums used to be accompanied by screaming at me. The quiet worried me. One hundred years amounted to more than a small amount of time for dragons, but I was sure I'd known her better than that.

I was wrong.

"I remember trying to rip your heart out," she whispered below human hearing. She faced the window, staring outside.

"As do I."

"The urge to watch it stop beating was so strong I couldn't fight it."

Her own version of an apology. She'd take it back if I acknowledged it.

"Who do you think was behind it?"

She slowly turned her head, lifting her long red hair off her back. Incredulous best described the look.

I had to suppress the desire to laugh. I failed. As the laughter tumbled from me, I felt an easing of a century-year-old wound. "Stupid question."

"Either you're more naive than when I left, or just baiting me." Her lips twitched up for a moment.

"Obsidian and Nitha. Two demons with close to a cartoonish villainous streak."

"I wish they were cartoons." She toed the floor. "I'm glad you survived."

"That's nice to hear."

"I'm not trying to get back together with you."

I would take her back in a second.

"Understood." She was the smarter of us in emotional matters.

"Each time I see your face, I flash back to that night."

Even now, looking at me seemed to trigger pained expressions.

"It took me a while to replace that image with one of us making love."

A few decades, at least.

"We're on autopilot. Did I hear an apology?" Wretch's timing proved stellar.

Tanith stared at him and waited. She made him uncomfortable; unafraid, she rarely acknowledged his existence. It irked him.

He'd seen us having sex dozens of times. Wretch showed up whenever he wanted, including the middle of the night. At first, I had some performance issues. That wore off after a year. I knew he did it on purpose; so did Tanith. The last time, she turned around with her back to me, staring right at him while she rode me. Her pleasure at his presence stopped the visits. He never told me why I shouldn't trust her even after I recovered, the assumption being the attack should've been enough.

"I'm calling George again." I dialed his number, putting it on speakerphone.

He picked up right away. "I'm standing behind the bar. Elise is seated here, unable to figure out how I knew who took Angie. Even now, she's staring at me, amazed. Could she be this stupid?"

"Blonde, ditzy, smells delicious, with fangs?" Tanith asked.

"Uh, yeah," the gorilla shifter replied.

"It's not a fake. Part of her brain got fried when her human mother died during delivery. She's Kragen's daughter. Dammit, I should've known. She worked at the front desk of the gym. The owner, a werewolf, fell for her pity job until my boyfriend went missing. She didn't turn up for work after that."

It started to click for me. "She showed up in New Orleans the same day you did."

Greg came back dressed only in jeans. My ex-fiancée's eyes gave full approval.

He didn't notice, as usual. "Did I hear that right? Mr. Demon Drug Dealer, the new Arcane Court member, sent his brain-damaged daughter to New Orleans? What is up with demons? Can't we get a week without an invasion?"

Wretch answered. "No, they've wanted New Orleans for centuries. Access to the Mississippi with warehouses on the water's edge is perfect for import and export. Laythe kept Kragen out. This has less to do with my family, at least so far, than his desire to run us out of town and take over."

Beeping from the cockpit got his attention. "We'll be landing in a couple hours. Figure out a strategy."

"Does he think he's the boss?" Tanith asked me.

"No. We're partners. He knows who the supervisor is. It gives him greater freedom to fuck up and have me answer for it," I replied.

"That sounds more familiar." She forced a laugh.

We'd go to the club, grill Elise, and leave her fate to Wretch. Greg and George would hunt for Angie while I went after Grace. I knew Tanith wouldn't sit still, so she'd be with me.

The werewolf's phone rang. "Yes, sir."

Dale.

There was an angry alpha on the other line. He held the phone out so we could hear.

"…did you know how hard it was to gain their trust? Ruined in one damn night. It's a fucking good think the new Chief is a wolf or we'd have police riots. Is Cim there?"

"Right here," I said.

"Grace showed up here, beaten and bloody. She'll survive. You trained her well. She has skin under her claws we need to test without Angie, who's still missing."

I hoped Wretch didn't hear that. "We'll be there in under an hour. Send a couple of your best to the club. George has Elise, Kragen's half-demon kid there. She's involved."

The sounds of wolves howling filled the plane. "On it."

Chapter Fourteen

Wretch landed the plane with a thump, running through the door to get us before we stopped moving.

"Let's go," he barked.

We got our things together as the door opened. Wretch shifted. "Who the fuck is here?"

"Hello, Uncle Fester. Nice to smell your diseased ass. Do you ever take a shower, or do you count on being too foul for maggots?" Grace's voice shook as she leaned heavily in the doorway.

Greg rushed to her side, catching her as she wilted. "You shouldn't be here."

"You are new." She patted him on the head.

I had to laugh. Wretch joined in, leaving Tanith confused.

Grace peeked over the wolf's shoulder. "So this is the hot lady who had your panties in a bunch?"

That made my ex laugh. "He doesn't wear panties. But yes, we get under each other's skin like no other." Her eyes focused on me. "I assume that still stands."

I nodded. The rest of my body tensed.

Dale's arrival blocked the light from the doorway. "We need to move."

He backed out, followed by Greg carrying Grace. I picked up our bags, holding my hand out for her. It felt natural. Wretch made gagging sounds as he followed behind us.

Dale filled us in on the ride to the club.

"Grace found where they took Angie. It's a small house, New Orleans style, with one hallway running from the front door to the back. My scouts are there now. It appears they want her research."

"At my house," I said. "They don't know she keeps it in my basement. They'll think it's at the morgue. How's your guy there?"

Dale nodded. "He's fine, said they haven't come by, but he does have a conference in a meeting room today. It's full of cops in and out of uniform."

"They won't know who's armed. Good." One thing in my favor.

Wretch seethed in the corner. "I'll get her out."

"It's a trap," Grace said, reaching for him. "They want you, and Cim. When they get the research, they'll come for Greg and George. Don't make this easy for them, please."

He kissed the back of her hand. "You and Angie. The only two women who can calm me down and after this, I'm sending Angie out of town."

I'd never heard his heart break before. It made me uncomfortable.

"Never, ever, did I think I'd see this," Tanith stage-whispered. "Wretch, you're in love."

"Yes, you bitch. So was Cim the night you tried to remove his heart."

"I was drugged. I apologized." Her hands shook in her lap.

He'd found a new target for his pain. "You didn't check back that week, month, or next thirty years. What was it like in Thailand with my grandmother? Did you cackle over your accomplishment? Plan the next attempt on our lives?"

Venomous rage spilled from Wretch.

Grace pulled away, fearful. He noticed, trying to pull back.

Tanith spoke quietly. "I went to my parents in Scotland. Away from human contact for ten years, I regained my senses. My mother fed me herbs until I stopped hallucinating. Did you expect me to call?"

"Enough." I was done. "Drugs did that and now this. Let's go after Kragen first, then your grandmother's DNA operation. Okay? Focus."

The rest of the ride happened in silence. George stood behind the bar with a smirk on his face.

I dropped our bags, waving to the rest to sit in the large booth up front. Seated in the back, hidden from public view, was Elise, her lips sewn shut magically by the demon seated next to her. A woman I didn't recognize, but Wretch did.

"Iona." He gasped.

His mother was alive?

And here?

"Care to explain?"

"She's been in hiding for four hundred years. Only Nitha knew my mother survived the deadly attack after I was born. Not even Obsidian knows." He walked slowly to his mother, like afraid she'd vanish if he moved too fast.

"Obsidian found out yesterday." Iona pulled her son into a hug. "How ya doing, boy?"

"Boy?" Grace burst into laughter. "To think, I've been calling him Uncle Fester all these years."

"He loves that, by the way," Iona replied. "I heard you might need a hand with Kragen."

I stood still, stunned into silence. I understood Wretch's keeping this from me.

Offering my hand, I introduced myself. "Iona, I'm Cimmerian, the Death Dealer. Tanith is a dragon and my ex-fiancée. This is Grace, a jaguar shifter who runs this bar; Greg, a werewolf your mother injected with demon DNA, and behind the bar is George. He was born human, but after DNA injections by your mother and stepfather, Dr. Brun, he shifts into a lowland gorilla."

"You're the beast who stuck my mother into a wall?"

George looked embarrassed. "Yes, ma'am."

"Thank you. Laythe deserved better." Sadness crept into her expression.

Wretch's worries multiplied by the hour today. "Why are you out in public?"

"Kragen found out I'm alive. He sent this little bitch." She glanced at Elise. "Besides, it's time for me to play along with you."

"I need a drink," I said, heading for the kitchen.

Grace followed me. "It's crowded in here."

"That'll change. Wretch will take his mother home with him. Tanith will need a place to stay, and Kellen will be here in a few hours."

"You're overstaffed, boss." She poked me.

I pulled her into a huge hug. "No. I'm not." I held on as she struggled.

Breaking free, she waved her hand in front of her nose. "Bathe."

"Alcohol."

She took the bottle from me. "Upstairs, there's enough of your stuff left. Get cleaned up. If you go looking for Angie tonight, they'll smell you coming."

Tanith joined us. "She's right, you stubborn ass."

Grace laughed and draped her arm around my ex, pulling her back to the bar. Suddenly, a shower sounded good. I took a bottle of rum with me, downing half on my way upstairs.

Tension fell away from my shoulders. Grace was partially correct. I now had a full team. Fighting Kragen would take everyone downstairs, plus Dale and Aaron feeding us information. Second time Angie had been taken in weeks. She needed to leave town, permanently. Humans made better targets—they folded under torture. Shifters' pain tolerance included moving bones and organs around.

Soapy water washed down the drain as I tried to take it all in. Iona lived. While she was a great fighter by reputation, with an appreciation for male demons, Obsidian would come after her daughter.

Stepping out of the shower, I stood eye to eye with Wretch's mother. The intensity of her glare sent my penis looking for a way back into my body. I'm pretty sure I heard a squeak as my ass squeezed shut.

"Ma'am."

"You take care of my son." A demand.

"Yes, I do."

She blinked. "He loves a human woman?"

"He'd rather not."

"She's missing."

"For the second time in weeks. If she survives this time, he'll send her away."

She nodded. "I tried to send his father away. He's dead. Angie needs to move far enough away that my son can't track her down. We don't love lightly in my family."

As long as I had her with me, I decided to ask a few questions. "If I may. Why did you stay hidden even after Nitha started stalking him four hundred years ago?"

"He told me to stay away. When you showed up, I knew he'd be fine."

"Flattery helps, but I'm still suspicious."

She nodded. "You should be. Where do you want me?"

"We have too many appendages, again. I'd prefer you leave and take my ex-fiancée with you." Angie's kidnapping reminded me how much better we were as a duo.

"Will she come willingly?" she asked, a raised eyebrow the only acknowledgement of my nudity.

"No. But it will be fun to watch." I tried to hide a laugh.

"You need to find out who Luke is. He's letting this happen. Laythe would've found Kragen and shredded him for this intrusion," she said. "I'll take anyone you pick to my safe place until you give the all clear. It's well defended."

"Who else knew you were alive?"

"Only Wretch. Laythe thought my place was raided when they moved here. I left it that way. Maybe if I'd come back, we could have killed Obsidian." Regret filled her voice as she lowered her shoulders.

I'd loved Laythe, too. I'm sure Iona knew that. Her not mentioning it made me like her more.

She went back downstairs as I got dressed.

I missed lazy days. "Fuck."

"No." Grace stood in the doorway.

"You look like shit."

She laughed, pulling me into a hug. "At least you don't smell like demon blood anymore."

"It was nasty."

"Care to tell me what we're up against?"

"You are going with Iona until it's safe."

Letting go, she gave me a look I knew well. Then, she sighed. "I'll go only if Iona teaches me to fight. I'm not any good here if you, Wretch, and George have to protect me."

We walked downstairs to a quiet club. Elise sat silently in the dark, taking mental notes. I didn't want to kill her, not yet. Her presence put us in jeopardy.

"Where can we stash her?" I asked Wretch. His security cameras all over the French Quarter would allow us to see if she was missed.

"I say we let her go," he said with a skull-splitting demon grin.

"I'm listening." Getting a cup of my favorite tea, I glanced over to see Elise mouthing the names of the ingredients. "She's under a communication spell. Sending our words and motions back to Kragen in real time. Who took the spell off her lips?"

Wretch growled. "I did." He shifted back into his devil-in-a-smoking-jacket look.

"I've heard enough," Iona said. She walked over to Elise and pulled her jaws apart.

Elise's body slumped as Iona spun her head until her spine snapped. "Demon bitch."

"She was half-human," Grace said, covering her mouth.

"Fiction. Kragen spread that rumor to protect her. She's full demon. Or, she was," Iona replied.

The demon soul screeched as it exited her body, wriggling in the air with fury before vanishing.

I looked at Wretch.

"She said Kragen would get another body for her and this time, we wouldn't recognize her." He tried to look nonchalant, but he sounded worried.

Holy fucking shit. "Another body?"

Iona sighed. "The drugs Kragen peddle slow down the decaying effect so pure demon souls can stay. The new body can last for months."

"Human bodies can't handle it." I knew what she'd say next. Yet, I hoped I was wrong.

I wasn't.

"He's used shifter bodies for centuries," she replied.

Grace rolled her shoulders back. "You need bait?"

"Whoa, girlie. Not you." Wretch protested. "You stay you. Always."

"Aww. I wanna gag." George tried to break the tension. He ignored the look Grace sent him from across the bar.

I really liked him.

"I need to go." Iona hugged Wretch. "Grace, you're with me. We'll be safe."

Tanith looked around the room, carefully studying the expressions. "I know I should leave to protect them, Cim. I won't. I want this prick as bad as you do."

"I'll go with them," Kellen offered. "A dragon's skills might be needed, and I could teach Grace self-defense and demon fighting moves."

"A strong dragon male. Just my type." Iona winked at me.

Wretch almost came out of his skin. "No fucking way. Don't you touch my mother."

Kellen grinned. "You want a brother or a sister next?"

"Who has Vegas?" We couldn't leave it unattended.

"I'll call the Court. They'll have someone new out there by tomorrow. I wanted to be in the middle of this fight and I can't do that while watching an entire city of gamblers." He stood taller, like he expected me to argue.

I couldn't. In the Court's eyes, we were equal. Honestly, he was the best fighting teacher for Grace, other than Wretch or myself, with also the added bonus of knowing Wretch would stew about his mother curling up with another dragon. I would enjoy this.

Iona vanished with Grace first, returning after Kellen made a phone call to pick him up. Standing at the bar, I looked around. George tried to look busy behind the counter, Greg headed to the kitchen shouting something about needing meat, Tanith looked hesitant, and Wretch downed a bottle of liquor. In one gulp.

"Worried Mommy has found a new scaly partner?" I asked, ducking as the bottle flew over my head.

"Fuck you."

"Oh, you wanted me to offer?" He spelled my mouth closed. I raised my eyebrows.

Tanith laughed. "You have to teach me that spell, creepy."

He looked at her critically. "I won't teach you a fucking thing."

"Still pissed?" This time, she didn't drop her head in shame.

Wretch shifted back to demon dandy human. "I hate you for what you did. I was your biggest supporter. Even when he doubted you, I didn't. So yeah, I'm pissed. You were a plant. You still might be working for my grandmother."

"Is there a way I can prove myself?" Her mouth twitched.

I felt the spell on my mouth release. "Wretch?"

"Yeah," he answered. "It'll hurt like you're being burnt from the inside out."

"I'll do it." She started to strip, causing a gathering of men outside the window.

George cursed, walking to the front door. "Hey, you want to stare at me?" He dropped his pants. He'd gone commando that day.

The men walked away, one lingered a bit. Seemed he liked his men beefy and gifted.

George came back in, pants still unzipped.

"Does that come with a kickstand?" Tanith asked.

That's when he blushed. He wasn't confident around women. "Yes, ma'am?"

The last time women reacted to his body, we'd been leaving the cabin after killing Narran to end his human dismemberment operation. The reporters, EMTs, and a few cops had whistled at him. He'd had no idea how to react.

Wretch spewed alcohol and burst out laughing. "Tan, he doesn't know how to take a compliment."

"Wet behind the ears," she guessed.

"Among other places," Wretch said.

"I'm right here." George cleared his throat. "I'm not a Lothario like you, Wretch. That doesn't mean I'm inexperienced in bed. I'm picky. I had to be since I can crush a human woman if I don't pay attention." Then, he looked right at my best friend. "The women I sleep with also have guns. I can't survive a bullet to the brain."

My turn to laugh. In fact, I had to sit down. Wretch grumbled as Tanith looked confused.

"Tan." I hadn't used her nickname in a century. "Wretch's human girlfriend, the one who helped you this morning, emptied a gun into his head when he shifted mid-orgasm."

Her laughter filled the room.

"It's damn near midnight and we need to find Angie." Wretch vanished.

I answered the question hanging in the air. "His private surveillance system will find her. I'd be surprised if he didn't have a trace on her. Otherwise, he'd have vanished the moment we got back."

"I wondered at the delay," Tanith said. "Can I get a drink, or something to eat?"

George bowed. "Anything you'd like. Until we know if we're kicking ass tonight, we can keep it non-alcoholic."

"Someone mention food?" Greg pushed a kitchen cart past the bar with five steaks, a bowl of fries, and a loaf of bread.

"Thanks, Greg," I said, sitting down.

George filled two pitchers with water, setting them in the center of our largest booth table. A calmer inside meant more demons came by. The place filled up with George and Greg taking turns mixing drinks and pulling food from the back.

"Grace stocked up the cooler in case there was trouble," George explained. "She said we'd be able to keep this place going for a month without her."

"How'd she know?" Tanith asked.

I answered. "We're pretty sure she was going to return to the Yucatan and marry her boyfriend. The stock pile says we were right."

"Smart girl."

"She's like a daughter to me," I said with a warning glance.

Tanith nodded. "Got it. Sharp one, then. Even seems to have escaped Wretch's bedroom."

He picked that moment to return. "My bed? What about my bed?"

I glared at him. "Grace."

"Declined the offer. Then Cim here let me know any advances would be met with repeated penis loss until I couldn't shift a new one."

"Angie?" George sat down.

Greg took payment from the other tables and sat down on my other side.

Wretch inhaled. "Dead. Her ashes with the rings she never took off were in my mailbox." His face had grown pale.

Oh, shit. She was dead. My heart hurt. George put his food down. This was big.

The last time he thought she'd died, it had been ugly. "If you lose it, I'll kill you myself."

"She left me a note." He held up a tattered piece of paper. His hands shook as he held it in front of his face.

Tanith reached over and took it. "I didn't know her. I can read it without losing it. You okay with that?"

He thought about it. "You still okay with me burning the truth from your soul?"

"Yes," she said without hesitation.

"Then read." Wretch got up and walked to the liquor. Tonight, he'd spell it to get drunk.

Tanith's Scottish accent spoke Angie's last words.

"Wretch, you poor lost, lonely soul. I know you love me. More than you've allowed yourself to love anyone, other than Cim. I love you, too. If you're reading this, it means something happened, again. I knew the danger when I met you. I accepted it when I found out what and who you are. I've had an amazing ride with you and Cim. I'll say hello to Adam and Mike for you. We'll be pulling from the other side. I have only one request. Find love, my beloved. You deserve a woman, a non-human woman, to fight by your side and own you in bed…" Tanith paused.

Wretch lowered his head. "I had one."

She continued. "If you don't, Cim will never find love again, either. He's waiting for you to be happy first."

I thought it was a secret. She was good.

"Cim?" Wretch asked.

"Yeah."

"Can we kill a lot of people now?"

"In the morning. First, we get drunk."

"In her lab." He vanished.

I'd lost my appetite, so had Tanith, who'd teared up while reading. The other two finished the food and started to clean up.

George rested his hand on my shoulder. "Please go home and make sure he isn't beating himself up that in the former dungeon."

"Dungeon?" Tanith asked.

"Long story. Let's go." It would be a long walk. I needed the air.

We turned right out of the door, walking past the French Quarter Market.

"You've built a new family." She tucked her hand into my arm as we wove our way through the streets.

"Angie was part of it."

"Tell me about her." Her interest made me feel better.

I laughed. "She and Wretch met at a crime scene, I think. She was the coroner for the city, and he'd showed up to interrogate the demon soul she couldn't see. It hung over her head for thirty minutes, taunting him, before leaving. She was ordinary looking by human standards—normal height, a little chubby, brown hair and eyes. It was her laugh that got him. Each time he tried to intimidate her, she laughed at him."

"I need to say something."

I felt her grip tighten. "Yes?"

"I'm so sorry about your heart. Both trying to remove it and breaking it."

"Wretch is going to put you through the truth spell. Anything I need to know before I hear it from him?"

"You know it all. I stayed in Scotland. Your mother warned me about coming back. It took me weeks to recover from the drug. I'm not over what I did. Or you. How do I still miss you after a hundred years?"

"I'm a charming, fucking prick."

She laughed. "No, that's not it."

"Tan..."

"I'm not ready to start up again, either. Just putting it out there. It will come out during the spell." Letting go of my arm, she walked next to me.

"Thanks." The hole in my heart healed up. A hundred years of frustration and pain gone in an instant.

The rest of the walk was quiet, the ladies across the street long asleep. I wouldn't be surprised if they had cameras.

Wretch sat on the floor of Angie's lab. The slab where his grandmother had chained him to the floor to die still had blood on it. "She's really fucking dead."

"Maybe we get the werewolf coroner in here to clean up."

"No, she died because she sent the Court her findings. A human isn't allowed to know about us, much less test us."

"The Court killed her?"

"Vex. I'm hoping that's my last living grandfather, because I'd hate to kill three."

"No, you wouldn't. No burning this one on my roof, either."

Tanith looked at me as I heard George and Greg in the kitchen. Probably still hungry.

"Go up to the kitchen. The boys can explain it all."

I watched her go before turning to Wretch. "Vex did it himself?"

"No, he called a few minutes ago. Said he'd send me the video so I could see she didn't suffer."

I expected him to lose it. Go crazy, run around, shift a dozen times, or something. He didn't. He skipped the other grief phases and went straight to acceptance.

"Do you believe him?"

"I haven't decided. All I know is that my family can't hurt her anymore. Now, I get the human phrase 'going to a better place.' Even without an afterlife, she's safer than ever before."

"I know."

He glanced at the ceiling. "Tanith?"

"Still willing to take the truth spell." I'd seen it in effect once. She'd suffer.

"She should be with my mom, not us."

"Remember the last time you tried to force her into something?" I laughed.

"If I wasn't a demon, I'd still have scars. She's almost as good a fighter as you."

I pulled him to his feet. "Eat, sleep, plan."

"Drink, curse, eat, sleep, kill everything in sight." Wretch sounded almost normal. The glint in his eyes worried me.

Tomorrow would be interesting.

Chapter Fifteen

We'd gotten an early start at the club and moved the planning session to the warehouse.

Greg burst through the door carrying a case of energy drinks. "They're behind me."

Wretch and I stared at each other for a moment before we heard the shouts from outside.

"Your bodyguard brought them to our place?" Wretch's eyes twinkled in the light from the television.

We'd monitored the news stations for any violence or break-out of psychosis in the area. All was quiet; even Dale called saying the wolves could find so little going on that they worried.

George and Tanith had remained in the club, listening. I'd placed a call to Aaron who told me Drake pulled out of the poker game we'd discussed. He'd call the club if he needed to find me.

A river breeze carried the smell of nervous demons. "They're scared."

"They should be." Wretch cracked his knuckles while Greg dropped the drinks on the table.

"I mean, someone frightened them into coming here. They stink." Kragen had that effect, even on his most loyal henchman.

Shifting to dragon form, I stepped toward the door, grateful we now owned side-by-side buildings. If it got too rough in here, Wretch could transfer them next door where Dr. Brun had tied down children to inject them with demon DNA.

A smell hit me like a concrete fist slamming into my nostrils. Through watery eyes, I saw four demons run at me in full gangster costume. There must've been a memo.

They skidded to a stop three feet away.

"You're crying. Are we hurting you?" He pulled a 1940's machine gun from behind his back.

"Did you get lost on your way back to the set? Or did your boss think mob guys still look like that?" My eyes began to clear up. "Your stench is unique. Demon shit plus flop sweat. Did someone crap their pants?"

The guy with the gun waved it around. Clearly, he'd never used one before. His finger wasn't on the trigger. "We were in a bar, you stupid lizard."

Wretch made gagging noises while Greg wiped his watering eyes.

This group wouldn't live much longer. I needed to get them talking. "How did you get into a bar full of humans?"

"They fainted." The vigorous anger that powered them over here evaporated.

I remained on alert. "Why the fuck are you here? To whine?"

"Our boss would like to meet with you and Wretch. At the warehouse, in an hour."

Wretch walked up beside me. "An ambush invitation. Can we turn that down?" His grin looked huge.

"I don't think so. Do we get to kill these idiots? Killing the messenger is my favorite demon game." I tapped my toe claws on the concrete beneath me.

He raised an eyebrow. "You know it's a good day when demons shit themselves."

I was beginning to think neither Kragen nor Drake Kane were in town.

Wretch stared at me, focusing while failing to prevent a smile. I couldn't figure out why until Greg stepped between us.

The werewolf rolled his shoulders back as if he'd take me on. "Let me take these boys on."

The wiry demon leaned forward, keeping his body turned toward the exit door. "Kane wants to welcome you back from Vegas."

"Is he planning to run?" Wretch asked me.

I laughed. "He wants to get out before we tear his head off."

A growl came from Greg as he shifted in an instant, leaving both Wretch and I blinking while he tackled the demon with the gun.

The leaner? He'd reached the door. Wretch vanished.

That left two for me. "Which of you wants to play first?"

Neither of them would stand out. Short, normal builds, with close-cropped hair, and they'd shifted their eyes to brown. I'd seen them before, in poker games.

"We have to leave you alive. Kragen wants to see how you do on the drug," one of them said, shifting into jeans and a tank top.

I stopped moving, wondering if he just gave away a big secret. A closer look told me he wasn't at full capacity. "Your gangster days are over?"

"Humans can't report us to the were-cops if they only remember our costumes."

"Because the ugly suits hide the smell?"

He swung at me while his friend lunged at my right side. I punched straight out with my right arm, collapsing the demon's head. He froze in place.

We'd seen this before. Now, we knew it was Red Lady. "Wretch, we have more strangeness in here."

I heard a grunt outside as he walked back in holding the demon's head, skull, and spinal cord in his hand. "I have a talker, Cim. Seems we're on Kragen's hit list after Vegas."

"Well, does he think we went there by accident?" I grabbed the head of the demon punching my rib cage. It came off with a simple twist.

The head in Wretch's hand screamed. "We vowed to the Demon God we'd bring in the Death Dealer and you let him take your head? In seconds?"

"How many drugs are you on?" Kragen needed a better ground game.

It answered in a gurgle.

Waving my hand in front of the collapsed head, I could see his eyes follow but nothing else moved.

Wretch walked over. "You made a wax demon. If we collect enough, we can open a museum in the warehouse next door."

"There are more coming, you know. These idiots can't be the cavalry." I didn't want to mess up the warehouse. "How about next door?"

He nodded, grabbing the frozen demon and vanishing. I got a broom while Greg jumped on the head of his demon.

"You're going to smoosh him. Kill him so we can go next door."

His furred head lowered, he shifted back to human. "Sorry, I was having fun."

I had to laugh. "It's okay. Pop his head off so we can sweep up."

A howling scream rattled the metal walls, freezing Greg and me in place.

I dropped the broom as his demon turned to ash. We ran through the door, remembering to lock it, and then sprinted.

The door to the other warehouse stood open with foul smells rolling out like clouds. Greg's wolf nose wrinkled as he shifted. I expected him to puke in the river; proud when he didn't.

"What the fuck was that?" I heard Wretch shout over whimpering. "Are you trying to attract vultures?"

"Harpies," the head said as I walked in shifting, with Greg by my side.

I hadn't fought a demon in harpy form in four hundred years. Nitha loved that shape, especially when she hunted her family.

Wretch took the dangling spine in his other hand and pulled it from the skull. The soul wriggled into the air, vanishing in seconds.

"You thinking what I'm thinking?" Wretch's eyes were black.

"She's under protection." I hoped.

The screech of a banshee pierced my ears. I held my hands over my ears to protect them. Greg growled, leaping into the air.

Looking up, I saw three demons hovering over us. Two vultures and one harpy.

"Hello, Nitha. Who'd you kill to get out of your prison?" I wanted to call Iona and Kellen back. This was bad.

Wretch's psychotic aunt shifted into human form, landing on the concrete floor. "Kragen set me free. Seems he has a few profit margin problems."

She leapt for my throat as the other two dove for Wretch and Greg. I dodged her grasp, getting a hold of her legs as she flew by. Swinging her over my head, I slammed her into the concrete.

Bones cracked as she shifted into another human form. Small and dainty female attributes belied the strength and power of a thousand-plus-year-old demon.

"Let go of my feet." She stretched her arms toward me, lengthening them until she could scratch my hands.

Pain ran up my arms as she pulled on my scales. "I'm not letting go until I suck in your soul."

Wretch snapped his head around from his fight. He'd already won, but kept the demon alive for fun. "You have her."

The intensity of his glare hit me.

I dragged her around in a circle, spinning until she was airborne again. With all of my strength, I twisted her legs, smacking her body against the floor. The ground shook as a dust cloud rose.

She didn't make a sound. Greg, now in human form, took his demon by the head, twisting the neck until the breaking point. Then, he walked over to Nitha and waited for the air to clear.

"I want you to see this before Cim kills you," he said, killing the demon and offering me his soul. "You afraid of one hybrid?" Gesturing to Wretch. "How about a dozen or more?"

"Abomination!" Shouting, she rose from the ground, shifting into a snake.

The tail wriggled in my hands as she leaned over Greg. "It's been years since I devoured a wolf. You look tasty."

Her forked tongue smacked his cheek.

"Not today." He swiped at her head.

She dodged him as I pulled to get better leverage.

"Fly, you putz." Wretch stood there in a cloud of demon ash with his arms folded.

I'd remember the moment for decades to come. He knew it was the last time we'd fight Nitha.

"Shut up, Nephew. Did you see me kill your girlfriend?" Her words slurred from a snake's mouth.

Kragen had sent Nitha to kill Angie. It would hit my friend later. Now, we needed to survive.

Wretch dropped his arms, shifting into an eagle. "Let's play hunter and prey."

She moved back as he tried to get her neck in his beak.

Greg looked over at me. "Her last fight?"

"I hope." Shifting back to human, I started to spin in place, twisting her snake body like a rope.

The werewolf grabbed her tail two feet ahead of me. "I've got this. You take her head off."

Letting go was the hardest move I'd made in a fight. From there, I could've kept smacking her around until her skull cracked. Instead, I walked up to her head, shifted into dragon form, and sliced through her body.

She flopped to the floor, thick demon blood oozing out of the wound. Wretch stood over me, staring at her eyes.

We wanted to watch her life go out.

Nitha shifted into demon form. Part human, part goat; naked pink skin with tufts of hair scattered nonsensically. "I'll kill you, you fucking dragon. I should have killed you in your egg."

"Never stood a chance. My parents would've taken you out." Their reputation still kept the Yucatan Peninsula demon-free.

Wretch laughed, shifting into demon dandy. "She was talking to me, Cim. Even though I was born to a demon mother, my dragon father's genetics formed an egg in her body."

"She died protecting you," Nitha spat out, smiling.

The wound on her side didn't heal. "You took the drugs. The gash is still open."

"I made myself better," she protested. I'd never heard her sound afraid.

"Your life is over." I reached over, twisting her neck until it started to pop.

Wretch leaned into her face, saying, "My mother survived, you fucking bitch."

A furious scream flew from her mouth and I started to lose my grip.

"Keep screaming, my child. We can kill them all today."

Obsidian's voice sent a chill up my spine. "You're banished."

She cackled. "You didn't read the agreement. The demon council has declared it illegal as the local demon lord didn't sign off on it." Her voice came across as measured and calculating.

"Because you'd killed her." Greg shifted into a wolf, leaping to my side.

"Stupid pup. Do you think I'd sign my own banishment contract?" She pulled knives from her pockets.

At five-foot-tall, her human form with an Asian face and body movements wasn't as threatening. However, her skill with knives had left Greg with massive blood loss the last time they'd met.

"I'm done." I took Nitha's head, snapping her neck. "You have no more children."

Obsidian's pained expression surprised me. It seemed I'd killed the one child she loved.

Wretch grabbed Nitha's soul as it danced in the air. "Cim, you need a little more power to take on my grandmother."

I opened my mouth as he forced her protesting soul down my throat. Her anger filled me with fury as I swallowed her magic. The demon spines along my wings grew; pain along my spine told me those increased in size, too.

"Is this what you fear?" I knew the answer before her face twitched.

"Yes, it's what she fears the most." Iona appeared between Wretch and me. "I see the evil bitch is finally gone. Well, Mother, what's your next move?"

Obsidian's expression shifted from pained grief to anger to surprise. "You're alive." An accusation.

Iona crossed her arms. "If my father has his hands in this, I'll take him out, too. My child and his dragon guardian, the Death Dealer, aren't running from you. Understood?"

Obsidian laughed. "Can you take me and Kragen on, you worthless child?" Then, she vanished.

We waited for her to reappear. Ten minutes later, I let out my breath, shifting to human.

"Did we win?" Greg asked, changing back to human.

"Round two, yes." Wretch spoke the clothing spell for the werewolf and myself.

Chapter Sixteen

"The last time this happened we went home to find…" I didn't finish the sentence.

Wretch vanished as Greg and I locked the door, leading Iona back to the club. I unlocked a door that was open when I left, afraid of what I'd find inside.

Wretch shouted from my office. "Up here."

"Fuck."

Iona looked at me.

"The last time we won a fight with your mother, she left two werewolves in Laythe's foyer. In pieces."

"Oh, fuck." She took my arm as we ascended the stairs. "I left Grace up here with Tanith and Kellen."

Greg paced in the bar. I wish I could've stayed there with him.

Each step brought me closer to pain. Instead of rushing to get it over with, I savored the moments when I didn't know about whatever lied ahead.

"Get up here, you miserable, fucking dragon," Grace said.

I took the last few stairs in one leap, carrying Iona against my side.

Her hands shaking, she handed me a note. It read, "*This is for Elise.*"

I didn't see what he meant. Then Wretch moved out of the way, revealing Tanith clearly drugged and writhing in Kellen's arms.

"Please kill me, Cim. She's going to use me against you again. I'd rather be dead." Her voice carried none of the confidence I'd grown to expect.

My eyes filled with tears. "No fucking way. We'll figure it out."

"Bodies?" Greg asked from downstairs.

"She's drugged Tanith into psychosis and suicidal thoughts," Grace yelled back. "No body parts, puppy." She winked at me, knowing it would get him up the stairs.

Kellen cleared his throat. "I can help her heal in Vegas."

She lifted her arm to protest.

He ignored it. "We are all targets for Obsidian and Kragen. This hasn't changed today. In Vegas, I know the terrain and the contacts. The demons in the zombie demon parade can't be happy about being used. Cim, I'll fight there, with Tanith by my side. The demons we let gamble and play in the casino trust her. We can beat Kragen by chipping away at his demon workers. If she shows up, I'll text both of you. Wretch can get you to his suite in seconds."

"Damn, that makes sense," Wretch said, smirking.

"Fuck you, demon," Kellen replied.

My best friend laughed. "You know, there was a time—"

"Enough." I wanted to seal this pact and get moving on the next part of the plan. Nitha's death represented a huge step in taking down Obsidian. "Kellen, take Tanith back to Vegas. Make sure she lives through this."

"Cim, I can't do this." Her voice shook.

I felt for her. "You'll gain demon powers. Like Greg and I have now. It's strange at first, but gets easier to handle. You'll be able to smell demons before you see them. With Nitha gone, we've made Obsidian angrier, but she'll take it out on us. You're safer in Vegas. Even better, if you have a new boyfriend, she won't kill you to hurt me."

Kellen's gaze dropped down. That's when I knew.

"Okay, you two. Just don't get googly-eyed around me. I'm not used to Tanith being in my life again, much less gushy with another dragon." My stomach lurched. I needed to take a deep breath so I didn't barf on my own feet. "Wretch, we need to regroup. Too many appendages too soon."

He understood, nodding. "Thin the herd."

"Excuse me?" Grace placed her hands on her hips.

"We're vulnerable. Tanith and Kellen in Vegas helps. It's good, but I want better." Only I had no clue who to let go. Each member of the team offered a unique perspective.

"You're too nice," Iona said.

"I'm more evil," Wretch stage-whispered.

I nodded. "Who's making sure Obsidian isn't in New Orleans right now?"

"She promised," the werewolf said.

"The Court is dragons and two demons. You know who they'll send after her," I growled.

"Us." He chirped back. "I planned it that way."

I sighed, rubbing my forehead. "Did you always plan on death by granny?"

"What's up your ass today?" He poked me in the chest. "We killed Nitha."

I ignored the congratulations offered by those who weren't there. "You're willing to sacrifice us."

He bragged. "If she's marked by the Court, no demon will help her. My grandmother counts on her hideouts, minions, and lovers to keep her safe from us. Without them, it's you and me taking her on. We can beat her physically."

He must be fucking delusional. She hung werewolves in the air with her magic and sliced them with scalpels. I shivered at the memory.

"The demons are too familiar with the warehouse. It's compromised." George's voice calmed me. "In fact, the only place we've been safe is here at the club."

He was right. Damn, I needed a better plan, the death of Nitha not nearly as satisfying as I'd wanted.

"We need to check the mansion. She knows every inch of that place."

Iona looked confused. "Why do you live there?"

"It was Laythe's." It sounded weaker out loud.

She understood. "Let's go. I can spell it so my mother's DNA, alone, will trigger alarms. With your and Greg's powers—"

I raised an eyebrow.

"Grace knows a lot," she continued, explaining. "You'll be able to hear them. Living in a trap isn't the wisest idea. At least, you have, what? Four grown shifters living there?"

"Three. Myself, Greg, and George."

"Grace?"

The jaguar shifter grinned. "I live here. Upstairs, in Cim's old third floor apartment."

"This place is safe," I stated.

Wretch backed me up. "I don't know why, but this building is the safest in New Orleans."

His mother looked at him sideways. "Your house?"

"Comes in second. I have to entertain."

"Not right now, you don't," she said.

"I haven't in the past two months. It's been a bit busy. Then, Cim here got back to work and your family showed up." He tried to shift blame.

This was new to me. I'd never seen Wretch act like a child.

"Uncle Fester," Grace said, slipping her hand in the crook of his arm. "How about you transport Tanith and Kellen back to Vegas? Like now."

I'd looked away but apparently, they were getting cozy.

"Okay, you two. We're done here." He leaned over, placing a hand on each of their heads, and vanished.

"Do we get that power?" Greg asked.

"I'm not sure I want it." What if I showed up in a different shape?

Wretch showed back up, wet. "Cim, Greg, back to Vegas. Small demon infestation at the penthouse."

He touched us and we appeared in the living room.

"The lobby, by the elevator," Wretch said, walking away.

"I'm not sure that I'm good with vanishing and reappearing in another state," Greg said, shifting.

"Me either, friend." Also shifting, I followed behind him.

The group in front of us watched like it was their favorite television show. These demons came from the warehouse. They smelled of human blood, feces, and smoke.

I looked right at Wretch. "Roof."

He nodded, grabbing Greg and me, then vanishing. We appeared on the roof. Fresh air wafted by and I sucked it in, filling my lungs.

Greg tried to hide his gagging.

A few seconds later, Wretch reappeared with the three demons. "These idiots need air fresheners."

"Says the demon who lights his grandfather on fire on my roof?" I laughed.

He smiled, shoving the demons into the rooftop pool. "Chlorine might help."

"Only if they filled it with bleach, too."

The first demon crawled out of the pool in the form of an octopus, his suckers popping on the concrete as he made his way to Greg. The werewolf snapped his jaws around the leading tentacles. I wasn't going to tell him the demon could regrow them faster than real octopi; he'd need to learn.

The other two flew out of the pool as harpies—too many for me in one day. Prettier than demons in their natural form, hideous still didn't cover it. I'd yet to find a word to describe it. Wretch called it birth control. I had to agree.

Chlorinated water fell from above as the harpies circled. Greg's yell sounded more like a gurgle as the demon smothered him. I took three steps and started pulling arms off. It took the creature longer to regenerate as I threw parts of him across the roof. "Can't reform with bits missing? What was that? A necessary bit?"

Greg's muffled laughter irritated the demon who promptly dropped him and shifted into a man. Only he had one leg. Unaware of his disability, he leaned into a walk with nothing underneath him and face-planted. The ones above squawked while muffled cursing accompanied slow growth of a new limb.

"Next!" I yelled, looking up.

In the distance flew a helicopter. It swooped close as it returned from the warehouse area. I could see flashing lights from that direction. The investigation would take a while. No wonder these three ran away. We had dragons on the Vegas police force, with werewolf partners—necessary to hunt killers in the vast desert surrounding the city.

I hoped this chopper held paranormals; we were very much in full view with no way to pretend this was a movie set. The harpy above dove straight for the water, shifting into human form. The splash washed the other demon's limbs away from his crawling form.

A wave from the chopper let us know we were okay. Kellen would hear about this. He likely already knew. At that thought, he burst through the roof-access sliding glass doors in dragon form. It had been decades since I'd fought alongside another dragon.

Wretch caught my eye and shrugged. We had plenty of chances and gracefully stepped back.

Greg, who couldn't see him, jumped up to take on the demon squirming on the pavement. Kellen walked into the pool. The water around the demon turned yellow. It seemed the local talent had a serious reputation.

Kellen watched as the demon shifted into demon form, raising horns on his head with membrane wings on his back. He couldn't fly from where he was, the bottom of his wings submerged. Kellen waited. I walked to the other side of the pool, lowering myself in. I didn't want to spook this one. He looked like he was conjuring something.

Greg pulled his demon prey over to the gelatinous goo, appearing to be gentlemanly. The demon's grin gave away his assumption the wolf was suckered. As he reached out to reconnect, Greg growled, jumped on his chest, and ripped his throat out. The demon's soul hollered. The wolf ignored the sound as he gnawed at the neck until it snapped.

Then it happened. Greg pulled back, taking a deep breath, and the demon's soul infiltrated him.

"Aw, fuck. I don't want to kill him if he loses it." Wretch strode over to him.

"We may not have to," I said.

Greg stood up, dazed but definitely himself. "There's a dying voice in my head telling me to go fuck myself."

"You absorbed his soul?" the demon in the pool asked.

"My grandmother created more of you," Wretch said. "She's building an army whose DNA is close enough to demons to absorb our magic."

"You're all doomed." The water around the demon in the pool took on a definite red tinge. That was new. I nodded at Kellen and we both backed out.

In a blur, Kellen took off from a standing position, flew through the air, and re the demon with one hand.

"Nice move. You study karate?" Wretch joked but I saw the admiration on his face.

"I've been trained in all martial arts. My parents insisted," Kellen answered from behind me. Unwinded, he waited for the screaming soul to emerge. "Should I be offering this prick to either of you for a power-up?"

Greg laughed. "I'm not a character in a video game."

"You are from where I'm standing." The dragon's voice carried respect.

The wolf looked scared. I couldn't blame him. The repercussions would be tough. He couldn't go back to the pack after this. He, like me, would become more demon with each inhale of a soul. His demon DNA might make his transition faster.

Wretch and I didn't speak to each other about it. I would sit down with Greg and explain it, the only benefit I saw being the ability to eradicate Obsidian and Kragen with matching demon powers and shifter healing ability.

"I want to go home," Greg grumbled.

I nodded.

Wretch walked over to the door leading to the stairs. "Kellen, you need us for anything, text me and we'll appear in my suite."

The wretched soul squirmed its way into nothingness over his head as Kellen smiled. "I've got things here, Wretch. Tanith and I handle Vegas just fine."

"Now that I've removed the warehouse." It came in a growled statement.

"Yes." His pride wouldn't allow him to say more.

"If you and Tanith have become a target..."

"Agreed. I'll call in my family. They live close enough to visit every few months. A small clutch of dragons hanging around Vegas won't hurt."

I liked Kellen's family. His parents were over a thousand years old and ran an organic food store in the northwest. I should call my uncle. He ran the family in New York. I doubted the demons would go after him there, with twenty dragons living in the boroughs, but I'd been wrong before.

Chapter Seventeen

Whispering the spell for clothing, I walked back into the condo in jeans and a t-shirt.

I found messages on the land phone.

"*Come home now, we're overrun at your house.*"

"Wretch!"

"I got her messages, too. We're out."

I noticed Greg looking confused. "Grace's in trouble."

He nodded, easily passing Wretch and I on the way to the elevator.

"Wolf speed," I noted.

"With demon juice," Wretch whispered.

We might've created a bigger problem, but I wasn't going to be upset. A werewolf with demon speed would be a huge advantage back home.

On the elevator, Wretch grabbed us and vanished. Apparently, a snitch demon had showed up in the club—small demons, child-sized, who sat in corners, blending in and listening.

We appeared in the marble foyer of my house.

"A snitch demon?" Greg asked.

"We used to use them, too," I answered. "They have no allegiance. If you can pay their prices."

Wretch explained. "My family used them for centuries. Alliance with us got many of them killed, even after they'd collected the money and moved on. There are a few demon families who still hire them."

"Cim, where the fuck are you?" Grace called from the kitchen.

"Right here."

Pissed off was rare for Grace. "George has four demons stuck in the walls. We may need to knock the place down."

Wretch's head snapped around. "Obsidian?"

"That got his attention, didn't it?" The jaguar shifter snuffed.

I followed a growling sound from my living room. Greg ran upstairs and Wretch headed for Angie's lab in the basement, the last place we'd seen Obsidian planted into concrete by George. There was a demon stuck to the floor with a metal rod in my den.

"Been here long?" My grin exposed my teeth as I shifted them.

"That gorilla is nuts. Just kill me. Drink my soul, whatever. Make it quick before he comes back."

"How are you stuck?" He should shift and leave.

"He caught my spinal cord with the rod. It's stuck in the floor."

Well, I didn't know he could do that. He probably didn't, either. It did explain a demon remaining perfectly still.

"Punching bag?" Greg came in, winded. "Upstairs is clear. It doesn't look like anything is missing."

"Grace?"

"Haven't seen her."

"You watch this idiot. I'll check the living room, kitchen, and downstairs." I shifted to dragon form.

My talons clicked on the marble floor. I liked the sound. This was my home now and I wasn't going to give it up. The living room didn't have demons in it but one of the windows was broken close to the back. I went to the kitchen, also clear, and looked out the back door. It seems they came from the house behind us.

I heard Wretch's laugh as I descended. "We need the buy the house out back. It appears to sprout demons."

"I'm buying the entire block. I'm thinking eight-foot concrete walls around the edges and a wrought-iron gate with a security system at the driveway." He stood in the middle of the former torture chamber with a demon in each claw.

He'd shifted into his favorite demon form. More tufts of hair this time. He filled the room.

"You stink." Tears left my eyes.

"I made a dragon cry." He sounded too happy.

"Fuck you."

"We've already had that conversation today." These words coming out of a vampire-looking demon sounded wrong.

"I knew it!" The left hand demon howled. "I bet my friends you two were lovers. I win!"

"Do you think you're leaving here alive?" I plucked at his clothing with my claws.

A new smell filled the room. "I was only scouting the place."

"For who?" I leaned in, making sure he saw the golden fire in my eyes.

"A friend."

"You're brave." Or stupid.

"Yes, I am."

Ah, delusional. "Brave dies here."

"Uh. What if I tell you who hired me?" He bargained.

I stood up to my full height. "You think they're important enough to save your ass?"

The right hand demon coughed. "Not likely."

Raising an eyebrow, I waited. He didn't elaborate.

Left hand demon squirmed. "I work for Drake Kane."

The right hand demon huffed. "Weasel. He's a second class demon."

"Then why?" Noticing these two were not dangerous, Wretch shifted back to demon dandy form still with a firm grip on each.

They didn't try to run when their feet hit the ground.

The left one found some bravery. He turned to Wretch and took a swing. "Because he'll own this place soon."

Idiot. Wretch took his head off so fast, I didn't see how he did it. Bravado turned to dust floating to the floor.

We looked at the other one, now visibly scared.

"Kragen wants New Orleans. That's all I know."

"You're going to die telling us something we already knew." Wretch smiled.

The demon looked relieved.

"That one could've been helpful." I faked a protest.

"Fuck him!" Grace was behind me. "He tried to take advantage of me."

"And?" I kicked his dust with my claws. I wanted him to rematerialize so I could kill him all over again.

"No, Cim. He didn't get anywhere. I came by to check on the house. I used to stop by and see Angie when you were off being a hero." Tears soaked her face.

Wretch and I inspected her for damage.

"You realize that feels as creepy as your ashy friends there?" She froze in place.

"Sorry," Wretch apologized, looking genuine.

I tried not to look confused. "Yeah, I'm sorry, too."

"Bullshit! You'd strip me and get out a magnifying glass if you thought I'd gotten demon on me."

Protesting the truth would be futile. I shifted back to human with jeans and t-shirt.

"Did you two boys have fun in Vegas?" she asked, pretending to be okay.

Well, I'd heard enough and headed upstairs. I heard the hand vac behind me. Wretch was a neat freak.

"Don't you walk away from me," she said.

"Grace, there's a demon stuck to a floor upstairs, and I haven't seen George."

"I left him upstairs."

We left there and didn't see him. That had me worried. "You did that to the demon?"

"It was almost by accident."

"Almost?" I turned around as we reached the kitchen.

"I was aiming for his head."

"Kane." Wretch spat out as he appeared near us. "I'm sure he's offering rewards to anyone who can beat George. If that doesn't work, it'll be a death warrant next."

"How bad is Kane?" Grace got the whipped cream from the fridge.

I made coffee. Leaving the demon stuck to the floor gave me a perverse sense of power.

"As bad as my family but with better connections." Wretch pulled out a plate, filling it with crackers, cheese, and sliced pepperoni.

"I can smell that!" The demon in the den must be hungry.

"Can I kill him?" Grace stepped back as she spoke.

I filled the distance with anger, anyway. "No."

"I need to know I can." She was right.

"Fuck." Iona hadn't had time to train her. I handed her a machete from the back of the pantry door. "You'll need this."

"Normal people hang food there."

"I don't believe in normal." I'd never seen it.

Wretch got the snacks ready while we walked to the den.

"You can help me tremendously today," I announced.

His eyes lit up. Stupid demon. Greg tried to hide his laugh.

"She is going to kill you. Be good and sit still." I gestured to Grace.

He looked…well, horny.

Grace was gorgeous and deadly, my favorite combination. Yet, to me, she was a daughter. "Stop looking at her like that."

"Can we come up with a better way to kill me?" His eyes held slit pupils now.

Sighing, I looked at her. "Kill him."

Swinging the machete like her Mexican family taught her, she took his head off in one shot. "That's easier than clearing jungle."

"Yes."

"Oh, that's why you didn't want me to do it before. I might've taken the heads off dozens at work."

The machete fit in her hands. "Keep it."

"I'll put it behind the bar."

"Teach George to use it. Pinning a demon to the wall is handy. Killing one is better."

She swung it with an experienced arm. I went looking for the vacuum cleaner in the closet under the stairs. Closing the door with it in hand, I turned to see George and Iona at the front door.

"You left?"

"No." George looked nervous. "I was on the porch waiting for Iona."

"I need meat," Wretch said behind me. He grieved best over food. Too common an occurrence lately.

Adam, Mike, Laythe, and now Angie.

"Take me with you," Grace chimed in, holding his arm. "We need a steak dinner." Her first kill had made her happy. All my warning bells went off at once.

They vanished.

"Cim?" Her voice cut through my thoughts.

"Iona."

"We need to talk."

I smiled. "I only have those conversations with women I'm fucking."

Greg laughed from the kitchen.

"Grace killed?" she asked.

"Yes."

She nodded. "I'll stick close to town and train her. Women move differently than men. I'll stay enough away that it won't attract attention. I can train her in Wretch's gym. I assume he still gives martial arts classes at home?"

The last time we'd been in there, two demons had shown up. "It's not well protected. There's a street entrance."

"Who the fuck do you think I am? Just because I have tits doesn't mean I need you and my son to protect me. I've beaten my mother in hand-to-hand combat. If I train Grace, so can she."

"Sorry about the assumption. Tanith beats me in every fight and I've never pulled a punch with her. It wasn't a sexist assumption. I've not seen you fight." My defense sounded weak but sincere.

"Oh." She covered her mouth after the smile broke through. "How is Tanith?"

"Still a pain in my ass. Back in Vegas, fine with Kellen." It still made my stomach turn.

She laughed. "I put up the protection spell."

I walked to the den with the vacuum. Greg and George sat near the demon mess, each with a bottle of liquor in their hands.

Iona sat next to them, taking the bottle George offered. They watched me clean and lock up.

The broken window had a blackout curtain on it. I pulled it over. "We need a new window."

"I'll get one after food. I can install it." Greg stood behind me.

I could smell the liquor on his breath. Inhaling a demon soul had disturbed him. "You're handy."

"I'm a werewolf. We live in the wilderness."

Survival skills. I hoped I hadn't lost mine. Two hundred years in New Orleans and I'd adapted to the stench of beer and barf on Bourbon Street. At least, there were fewer smokers. Strangely enough, cigarette smoke burned dragon lungs. We didn't tell the demons. They could puff a pack at a time and it had no effect.

A faint scent of Drakkar lingered around the window. Demons' favorite odor cover. That, and Polo. I don't remember what they used before the 1980's, but it didn't work.

Greg honked the horn; he loved to drive. He was a good one, and now that he could absorb demon souls, he'd gain a larger mark on his head. I was stuck with him.

Locking the front door seemed futile at this point. Yet, I did. Wretch's idea of a concrete fence sounded good. I would be apprehensive until Iona's spell proved worthy. Seeing singed demon souls smoking in my backyard would be a great way to wake up.

We stopped on the concrete dock by the warehouse. Parking on Decatur Street wasn't a good idea. Walking across the tracks, I noticed three demons pretending to shop in the Market.

"Greg." I nodded at them.

He smiled. "Yeah, I can smell them. Do they think that works?"

"Maybe we should pick up beignets on the way?" George offered.

My stomach rumbled. "Huffing sugar sounds good."

"You aren't supposed to inhale it." Iona chimed in.

"Have you seen the pile she put on my plate the last time?" Greg asked.

I poked his side. "I think she likes you."

He caught one of the demons looking and winked at him.

I liked him more every day. "He's going to mark you."

"After Vegas, I'm thinking I will be, either way. This way, I enjoy it." He walked next to me.

We ordered our food. The staff at *Café Du Monde* knew us well. The powdered sugar piled high as the lovely lady behind the counter forgot herself staring at Greg.

"I don't think she's human," I whispered to him.

"Pack member. My status prevented me the last time. Now, my changes would affect our pups."

Again, knowing Wretch and I irrevocably changed a life. At this rate, we'd end up with our own type of pack. Hell, we already had that.

"Fuck."

"I'm okay with it. I didn't ask for the demon shots but they got me through junior high school as a skinny wolf in a pack of wannabe alphas."

Well, there was that.

Chapter Eighteen

The short walk from the cafe to our club was uneventful. Two demons pretended to shop while following us. New to town, obviously, since they didn't count on the crush of people weaving in and out of the open-air market. One step too close to fragile merchandise drew shouts from humans who wouldn't step back until the demons apologized or paid for damaged goods.

I liked the steampunk outfits one group wore. They reminded me of London. The smell of cooking beef hit me as soon as we walked in the door. We weren't alone; three full tables of drooling wolves sat along the front windows.

Greg headed back to the kitchen while I made a few drinks.

"Evening, gentlemen. May I interest you in a cocktail while the beef finishes cooking?"

I loved bartending—the reason why I bought the club to begin with. I could play with different combinations all night. Since shifter systems didn't allow us to get drunk, we had the added bonus of keeping our heads. A nice bonus with rogue demons running the streets.

My first night here, I saw a group coming from the corner. Probably walked over from the tracks, staying on the other side of the market so I couldn't smell them. Five young demons, all under a century, strutted into the club and demanded the 'lesser' species give up all rights or die.

They didn't expect me to laugh in their face, or for Wretch to appear behind me. He'd been upstairs ordering the construction workers to get our offices right. We needed floors that could bear the weight of our selves in every form, with friends.

The young demons' bravado slipped long enough for Wretch to spell them naked. The first time I'd seen it work. Since then, I've been spelled nude twice—once by a determined demon who wanted more children like Wretch, and the second time when second-rate demons at a poker game did it to me.

Which reminded me.

"Wretch!"

"What?"

"We need a wall."

"Fortress is already on order, Your Highness."

Kragen would poke at us for the warehouse operation. I couldn't stop his dealing. I'm not sure anyone could. Humans took drugs at a frightening rate. I'd settle for him going back to cocaine and heroin. Drugged shifters could get paranoid and go after humans. One werewolf pack could clean out a small human city in under a week.

With the added skills of Iona, and her training Grace, we might be strong enough to fight off anything Kragen sent into town. I needed to talk to Luke, the missing local demon lord, about policing his area.

My back was to the door when I heard the wolves growling. Turning, I saw a demon shift into a large bat flying at me. Three more demons appeared in the private dining area and headed for the wolves.

"Visitors," I shouted, hitting the button to lower the internal window blinds.

The demon's claws grabbed my hair as I ducked under him. Shifting to dragon, I couldn't expand my wings behind the bar. No light shone in the room as I heard Grace's footpads enter. She moved to my side, weaving between my legs.

They wouldn't know she was here, a black jaguar in a dark room. Her tail smacked me as she moved to the darkest corner.

Wretch appeared next me. "You're having a party without me?"

The wolves saw this and shifted, lunging at the demons.

"Don't break anything," was all I could say before my demon rounded back again. He'd spotted Grace and I wasn't going to let him go after her.

Walking to my right, I rounded the bar as he flew back. I needed to add ceiling fans. That would deter flying bat things. He swooped down toward me and I caught his wing.

"You can't fly without this," I said, yanking it hard enough for the membrane to tear.

He squealed.

Greg, in wolf form, walked from behind the bar, protecting Grace. She hissed at him. *That's my girl.*

Wretch decapitated the damaged demon, leaving the other two to the wolves. "You can't squeal. What the fuck is wrong with you?"

I dropped the other one who shifted into a bear, clawing at my face. "You're stupider than most."

This time when he changed form, I noticed a metal fragment stayed near his chest. "Are you wearing a spelled wire?" I knew they existed but hadn't seen one yet.

His cackle was an answer. Wretch smacked his head, vanishing with him. I heard a thud upstairs.

Grace hissed, shifting. I spoke the spell and she was clothed and put clothes on Greg as he changed. The wolves were at the table with two piles of ash nearby. I hit the switch to raise the blinds as Grace headed to the back for dinner. She'd vacuum after the guests left. Iona and George stood behind the bar which was now covered in an assortment of drinks.

"On the house," I said, gesturing.

The wolves thanked me as they helped themselves.

I walked up the stairs slowly. Whimpering sounds came from Wretch's office. The demon stood defiant. That pissed me off.

The demon's head bent back as I yanked his hair to his ass. Wretch pried his mouth open. Pouring diet coke, pop rocks, and Mentos into his stomach made me happy. His look of fear turned to terror as the combination began expanding his abdomen. I'd wanted to do this since I saw a video of the chemical reaction.

I let go and he fell to the ground, writhing in pain. His chest expanded as he fought to contain the explosion of gas bubbles. Waiting for him to shift, I noticed he couldn't. His body started to sound like a leaky pipe. Then, the smell hit. Gagging, I backed away. Demons didn't fart. I knew why. Holy hell, that was awful. Wretch's eyes watered as he leaned over our victim.

"Why don't you shift? See if all of your parts make it through?" Poking him in the stomach caused more leakage of air.

The sound of air freshener being liberally sprayed behind me let me know Grace had picked up the scent.

"Uncle Fester, what the fuck did you do?" She walked in with a towel over her entire lower face. "The wolves left."

I laughed. "Not taking any chances, are we?"

"I gagged. What did you do to him?" She didn't glance down.

"Pop rocks, Mentos, soda, and fear." Wretch poked him again.

A hole appeared in his side. I could see inside his body. The smell made my eyes water. "Close him up, that's disgusting."

"I can't. If he shifts, the damage spreads." Wretch glowed. "This is perfect."

"If by perfect, you mean, kills demons while gagging everyone downwind..." I heard the front door open.

Grace did, as well. "I'll get it. Vent this office. It's not like your customers have sensitive noses." She jumped down the entire staircase in one leap.

"She's good." The demon on the floor drooled.

Wretch bristled. "You look at her again and I'll put this mixture up your ass."

Laughing, I made my way downstairs. I needed air that didn't smell like sulfur farts.

The restaurant smells replaced the stench as I stepped into the bar. Taking a deep breath, I headed to the kitchen.

Grace hovered over a stew pot. "What the hell possessed you?"

"We wanted to know what it would do." I played innocent.

"Like school boys with toys."

"Well, we are. Minus the school."

"Minus the boys. You two are too old to be boys."

Wretch appeared, immaculately dressed and smelling of lemon. "Young at heart, my dear kitty."

Her claws clipped his jaw. "Don't call me that."

Rubbing his jaw, he smiled. "I felt like playing dangerous today. How'd I do?"

"You're a threat to stomach contents. No more," she announced, smiling as his face fell.

"That hurts, Grace." He feigned a heart problem.

"Your ego is stronger than Cim's dragon skin. Don't play with me." She put a towel back over her face as she left.

"She doesn't trust me." He winked.

"As most women you know, she learned early on you only take killing seriously." So did I.

"Our friendship. It's the only thing other than killing that I live for." He bowed, partly mocking, but his tone was serious.

"What do we know now?" The snitch and his friends had been an unexpected surprise.

He pointed upstairs.

"Only if you fumigated the place. That smell could melt wallpaper."

"Yeah, I cleaned the air out. Killed the snitch. I couldn't have him talking."

"Like there'd be a run on candy."

"Demons' need for eternal survival is strong enough to make a run on candy."

"Get him out of the building and no burning him on the roof."

"Decapitated and dusted."

"We've spent four hundred years battling your family. We need a new plan."

"Drake is small time but works for Kragen. We have a serious problem. If he wants New Orleans, he'll send in human and shifter addicts to run the streets."

I walked upstairs to my office. The smell was better but I still opened the windows and balcony door. Muggy breezes beat demon odors every time. "If he's making a run at us, he'll need more than his usual crew. Doesn't he keep fewer than a hundred demons on his payroll at a time?"

Wretch nodded. "Keeps the leaks to a minimum."

"He'll need more than that."

"If they're all here, he could do it, but his operation in Vegas requires at least half."

"Where else is he located?"

"Star Island, outside of Miami. He has a multimillion-dollar mansion alongside celebrities."

"Ocean access would allow him to get large quantities of drugs into the country." In fact, if I ran a drug operation, that's what I'd do. "We need more specific answers."

"I'll check my security cameras. Have you checked with Dale since we got back?" His voice trailed as he vanished.

"On it," I said, dialing my phone. If anything happened while we were gone, the tenuous relationship with the pack could dissolve.

"Cim, so nice to talk to you."

I heard a fight in the background. "Busy, Dale?"

"We found a few nosy demons wandering around the front yard. We've attached shock collars for Rottweilers to them. They don't learn," he said, laughing. "There are ten more circling the neighborhood."

I liked the new alpha. "We have a new demon lord assigned to the Arcane Court, a drug dealer. These may be his boys, checking out the new alpha. Or the invisible new replacement for Laythe is checking out the local talent."

"Seems the deal with Obsidian had side effects."

He didn't sound as upset as I'd thought he would. I took it as a good sign. "They may be working together. She showed up earlier but left quickly. It's a shaky truce. Demons don't forget centuries of rivalries because Wretch and I killed someone."

A howling sound followed by terrified screaming came from his end.

Dale laughed until he coughed. "Don't play with him. He's going to pee all over himself. I don't want demon piss on my flower bed."

It was all about priorities. "Can you hold them there? I'd like a chance to chat with your visitors." I flexed my fingers, extending my claws.

"Sure. I've never seen a dragon-demon fight."

"Really?"

"You're a rare creature, Cim. I'll clear out our basement; we use it to hold new wolves during the first few shifts. It should contain the fight and not alert the neighbors."

He made me sound like I needed a telethon. *Please save the endangered dragons. They hoard gold, rip the heads off demons, and inspire mythology and cave paintings.*

My mother would not only love it, she'd run it and make millions.

"Wretch, the wolves have a handful of naughty demons trapped in their yard with shock collars. Wanna play?" I knew my smile lit up my entire face. Also, it seemed we all had the modern equivalent of dungeons in our homes. Old habits.

My best friend clothed himself in black jeans, a black t-shirt, and pulled his hair back. Serious stuff.

"Hi ho, hi ho, it's off to kill we go," Wretch sang with a huge smile.

"You two need t-shirts that say 'Demons: pop off their heads and suck their souls'." Grace laughed. "Better yet, I want one. We can make it my official work shirt."

I had to think about that. There were friendly demons who spurned the 'kill all humans' mantra of their ancestors. Far more of them after Obsidian started experimenting.

The walk to Dale's would've taken thirty minutes. Wretch didn't walk into battle. He grabbed my arm and we appeared in the werewolf's main house. The sounds from the yard came clear inside.

"Nice entrance," Dale said, still holding his phone. "How do we get their friends inside?"

Smirking, I said, "We're here. They'll follow." I opened the front door. "Bring them downstairs. We're going to see how many of the others want to play."

The wolves looked to Dale, who nodded. They followed their alpha without question. It helped when things got ugly. In fact, Wretch and I would love to have that influence…if it wouldn't end up with our allies dead. I suppressed a sigh. Mike and Adam had been great friends and better werewolves.

"Did you bring Greg?" Dale looked for him.

"Uh, we didn't think about it." Wretch followed the collared demons down the back stairs.

"He's with Grace at the club. We had a small infestation of our own a little while ago. They're cooking dinner for members of your pack who helped us clean up."

Dale leaned in, whispering, "He's my nephew. My sister is his mother. Our parents didn't speak. He doesn't know, and I'd like it to stay that way until I decide it's time."

"I'll keep your secret. You do know Brun drugged him with demon DNA throughout his adolescence?"

"He told me after Mike and Adam's service. It's why he's happier with you."

"He's not sure he can be trusted." I knew that feeling. My absorption of demon power knocked my confidence around for fifty years.

"I trust him." Dale stood tall and proud.

I walked to the front porch and waited for the curious demons to approach. Four were in a beat-up car that had to run by magic. The muffler scraped the ground. Six more approached in two separated groups walking down the street.

"Gentlemen, I believe we need to have a meeting, don't you?" I growled the last. This was not an invitation they could turn down. "Should I call Kragen?"

That worked. Dale whistled and wolves came from the sides of the house. There was a gauntlet for the demons to get to me. They filed past, escorted by wolves down to the basement. I'd never been down there.

If we eliminated all of them, it would be easy for now, but Kragen would hit back and start a war. I wanted to prevent one.

"We can't kill all of them."

Dale understood. "My pups seem to like frightening them until they shift into demons. I can live with that."

"Wretch will have killed two or three by now."

"His reasoning?" Dale didn't know the entire history.

"His demon relatives have sent assassins, including relatives, to kill him for over a thousand years."

To a wolf, that had to be strange. "Family means nothing to demons." He spat it out.

We walked downstairs to find the collared demons being tormented by other demons. Wretch stood in a corner by a pile of ash. I looked around and it appeared he'd only killed one.

I held up one finger and he pointed at one demon getting the most enjoyment out of the game. Infighting was good.

Clearing my throat got their attention; shifting to dragon kept it. My voice raspy from the change, I said, "There's a segment of demons running drugs through gyms in Vegas. We blew up the warehouse. Is it a Kragen or Obsidian operation?"

The sadistic demon smiled. "Kragen's, with Obsidian's help."

Exactly what she'd told us earlier.

Wretch growled. "I'm going to kill every member of my family."

One of the collared demons forgot his predicament. "Not before we kill all shifters."

Taking the shock collar control from the sadistic demon, I approached the smartass. "Say it again."

He spit in my face.

I shocked him while removing his head with one swat. The collar stuck to my claws. It tingled. I loved my scales. "Anyone else?"

Seven demons looked surprised. The sadistic one stepped forward. "I can take you on," he said, shifting into a brown bear.

A good choice given the claws, but I'd fought the real thing. He took a swipe. I leaned out of the way, twirling the collar in my hand.

The blur to my left became claws on my wings as a demon jumped me from behind. The one in front of me swiped again, hearing his claws run across my scales instead of digging in.

I couldn't get to the one behind me; he started to tear my wings. Reaching behind me with my left hand, I grabbed a leg, pulling him. It tugged at my wing. He punched me in the side of my neck. Inhaling deeply, I smelled nervous dog and demon. The demon in the center stood back, watching.

Wretch laughed from across the room. "Cim, he thinks he's won."

Well now, I'd fix that. Stretching my wing moved him away from my body. Twisting, I swung my right fist into his chest. It left a dent. He wheezed, starting to turn yellow.

"Yellow?" Greg entered, nodding at Dale.

He must have texted him. Three demons moved forward, like they wanted to get involved.

Wretch stepped up, shifting into horned demon form, complete with forked tongue and tail. "That's dying demon yellow. All the fashion these days."

The sour smell of nervous sweat grew. None of the wolves flinched. They'd fought by his side before.

Greg's main focus was on the demon I'd hit. "Can he fix that?"

"Yes, if he can vanish and reappear." I waited, crossing my arms. Demons healed during vanishings while shifters did so during shifts. Same principle, different anatomy.

The demon had the same problem one had last week against Wretch. He tried to vanish but only a few parts came and went.

"Wretch, they're on Red Lady."

My friend glared around the room. "How many of you are on the drug? Do you know it prevents shifting when you're injured?"

No one spoke up but 'yes' bellowed in the silence.

"Well, this makes them easier to kill." Greg stepped in front of the struggling demon.

The sharp intakes of breath in the room let us know they understood. Obsidian would find it harder to recruit volunteers when this got out.

Greg looked at me. "May I?"

I bowed. "Please do."

His laugh turned to a growl as he shifted into wolf, leaping at the demon. The force of it knocked them to the floor. The demon ripped handfuls of fur from Greg's side. The howling sound echoed around the room as other wolves joined in. My head started to hurt.

Three demons vanished, including the sadistic one. He'd make sure the word got out. With his attitude, he needed to ensure his friends could back him up. The remaining four started to panic. Greg's demon wiggled beneath him.

"We can't have scared demons. What would everyone think?" Wretch tilted his head to the side, blood red eyes with goat-slit-pupils staring at each one in turn.

Dale patted my shoulder. "Pack, except Greg, head upstairs and make sure those three demons aren't out front. If you see them, ever again, kill on sight."

Now, there was room to move. Without a word, Wretch, Dale, and I each picked a demon to corner. They didn't cooperate. Two of them panicked, vanishing and then reappearing in the same spot.

I had to laugh. "New to this?" Reaching out, I grabbed the shorter one's head. It fit in my clawed hand.

"Do I need a rubber jar opener to twist your sweaty head off?"

The look of defiance on his face didn't fit the shaking and urine smell. He swung his right leg back and when he brought it forward, it had become an octopus leg. I'd seen this before.

"Wretch, what the hell is it with demons and octopi? You guys drown in water."

He bent his now snake-formed demon in half. "You can't beat those suckers for grip."

Suddenly, I knew what he meant as I fell over, dragged down by my leg. I'd released his head at some point. He leapt on top of me, pulling my scales.

"This looks familiar." I grabbed his waist with both hands and pushed until I felt bones shift. It had to hurt.

A grunt came from him as he resisted my efforts. Still yanking on scales, he would get through if I didn't kill him.

Splaying my right hand to the side, I stretched my claws to their full six inches. He glanced over, picking up his pace. As I sat up, he remained in my lap, continuing his work.

A bark told me Dale had shifted. His demon laughed until I heard gurgling.

I took my demon's head in my left hand and pulled it back away from me, slicing his spinal cord with my claws. The skin ripped in a jagged line. His movements didn't change.

"This is new."

"Fuck," Wretch said, snapping his demon's neck and stepping through the resulting cloud of ash. "He's still going."

"So they can't shift when punched but can fight without a head?"

"Hold on, Dale needs help."

I looked over. He had the demon by the throat but hadn't bit through. He had the bite strength. These weren't normal demons.

Wretch twisted the demon's head, pulling it off with a pop. Dale spat out the blood as he padded over to me.

"It's not you, it's them." Mine started to slow down. "Hey, seems their batteries run out."

There was a huffing sound I interpreted as a wolf laughing.

The demon's head came off with a twist. I waited for his soul to emerge like all others, green and bitchy. This one was red, in the shape of a devil's head, and could talk.

"Eat me, Death Dealer. Let's see if you can handle this." He taunted me.

The image faded, leaving a trace of red mist. "That's new."

Dale shifted, sitting next to me. "It looks like the drug changes more than their bodies."

"I will have to make sure I only suck down the green souls." I made more than a mental note—a flashing neon sign reading 'danger.'

Wretch shifted back to human, spelling himself his normal slacks and a buttoned-down shirt. Dale eyed the outfit so Wretch gave him the same.

"That doesn't look right," Greg said, unsuccessfully suppressing a laugh.

The alpha's clothes changed to form fitting jeans with a short-sleeved t-shirt. He stood up, thanking Wretch. "That's handy."

"I've found it necessary," I said, shifting back to human and spelling my own jeans and shirt.

Greg poked Wretch, who clothed him. He may be able to do it himself soon.

"Let's get out of here." We'd figured out who was behind the drugs, blown up his lab in Vegas, and were taking out his crew in New Orleans. Yet, something lay missing. I could feel it.

Wretch knew me well. "What is it?"

"I don't know yet."

"Big?" Greg asked.

My palms itched. "Yeah."

"Dangerous?" Wretch's smile could be seen from space.

I couldn't believe he asked that. It's like he forgot how many demons we pissed off every year. I waited for it to click in his head.

Greg laughed, saying, "Always."

We walked back to my place. A few blocks from the French Quarter, it sat an hour's walk to anyone we needed. Laythe had planned her location well. Running through everything we'd learned, we knew we were in trouble.

We sat around a table in the dining room. Grace had found a picture of Angie to place in the middle. Surrounded by food and laughter was her favorite place. Grace had become her best friend in the last few years and Wretch had owned her heart.

Iona, George, and Greg went back to the house after the meal, leaving Wretch and me with Grace. The way it used to be. Fewer people underfoot made me feel in better control, even if danger showed up.

Grace's cackling laugh carried up the stairs as she told someone where to find me. The demon walked into my office to talk to me like it was normal. Above him stood a voluptuous woman. Demon eyes took up more of her face than proportion allowed; yet she made it work for her. Standing with his head at her waist level, back against her legs, was an informant. He'd been assigned as a carrier for her tits. They were the size of watermelons. That explained the laughter I'd heard downstairs. Grace's usual decorum couldn't keep up with this.

"You are?" I fought a smile.

"You don't need to know my name."

"Uh huh."

"I'm a tit demon, okay? Shrunk to half my size, sentenced to carry her boobs for a century." He was grouchy.

Wretch appeared off to the side. "Hello, Max."

"You fucking prick. How dare you say hello to me? Do you know what it's been like for ninety-nine years? *Do you?*" He stepped slightly forward as he yelled, allowing part of one large breast to slide onto his shoulder.

My friend crossed his arms and legs leaning against my desk. "Your sentence is up in a month. Why are you here?"

"I want your protection."

This should be good.

"From?" I tried to keep the amusement from my voice, failing miserably.

"Kane. I hear he's been poking his head around. So, you help me, I help you."

Wretch crouched down to look Max in the eye. "How can you help me do anything?"

"Do you think demons notice me down here? I hear everything. I know who Luke is. I hear you've been trying to see the demon lord." He stood proud. Well, he tried.

"Laythe's replacement; we already know," Wretch said waving him off. "Nothing new."

"Luke's been dead a long time." The woman, who we'd ignored until this point, spoke up.

Max smiled. "We have a deal?"

Wretch shifted, startling Max. "Do you agree to follow all Arcane Court laws and leave town immediately if you break one? Even if we don't find out?"

A binding spell. Nice work.

Max blanched. "Yes."

I stood to full height. "Who's Luke?"

"Drake Kane."

Oh, shit. I needed a drink.

Max left with assurances.

"That's trouble," I said.

Wretch laughed. "We are good at it."

"We need to find him."

"He's not in town. He won't even show up for a poker game at Aaron's club. We have some time. Let Nitha's death make him think twice about the position. As soon as he appears in town, we kill him. On sight."

"Agreed." I extended my claws, watching the light dance off the razor blade edges.

ABOUT THE AUTHOR

Graylin Fox is a fantasy, and suspense author and poet. She began writing poetry in 1993 with her first poem published in 1995. In 2008 her characters demanded a larger format and she began to expand her stories into the short fiction market.

She lives close to the beach where she practices psychology during the week. Her life is full of friends, family, and four legged furry creatures.

She can be found at GraylinFox.com.

The Arcane Court Series continues with *Shadowed Vengeance* in 2015 and *Fanged Deception* in 2016. Look for *Demon Child*, a short story set in this world at your favorite ebook retailers.